# Sioux Warriors

# Sioux Warriors
## A Western Double

### Levi Johnson Mountain Man Scout
#### Book Two

## Ash Lingam

WOLFPACK
PUBLISHING
— EST 2013 —

Wolfpack Publishing
1707 E. Diana Street
Tampa, Florida 33610

www.wolfpackpublishing.com

Paperback ISBN 979-8-89567-218-1
Ebook ISBN 979-8-89567-217-4

# CONTENTS

# SIOUX WARRIORS

# Sioux Warriors

## Levi Johnson Mountain Man Scout 3

*This book is dedicated to the Western Fiction genre and the men and women who create it.*

"But even with the inspiration of others, it's understandable that we sometimes think the world's problems are so big that we can do little to help. On our own, we cannot end wars or wipe out injustice, but the cumulative impact of thousands of small acts of goodness can be bigger than we imagine."

**Queen Elizabeth II,**
Christmas Message 2016

# EXCUSES

THE SIOUX INDIAN RETURNED TO HIS BLIND. HE HAD TO crawl up to the clearing. He shifted through the shadows, unseen by the White men, just before first light. He sniffed the air like a dog—he noted the aroma of coffee and frying bacon. His mouth salivated because he had gone for the whole day before and night without food. He hid in the blind and didn't make the slightest move. He knew predators sought out movement. If he stayed still, it would be unlikely that the mountain men would see him.

He was deep in brush and brambles. His face was a painted mask with tones of green and brown. He blended in with the vegetation around him. He sparingly moved to sip from a goatskin water bag. He watched as the mountain men went about their day, curing furs they had stolen from the Sioux rivers and streams. Last year, Chaska had sold many furs at the Rendezvous. This year there were fewer beavers, so they had to go farther to trap and hunt. His small tribe had to do without because of the White men living in the three cabins. They had beaver traps set out all across Black-water Creek. This had to change, and Chaska appeared to be the only one prepared to take action.

It was true that they needed to go deeper into the forest to hunt, but Chaska could have gone in any other direction. He chose to follow this path not only to throw the White men off their land but to get restitution for the death of his brother, Black Bear. He was killed by a mountain man who they called Blade. He knew he would be easily recognizable because his brother had supposedly severed his arm in a battle.

The same battle that cost his younger brother his head. The White man with yellow hair cut it off with an Army saber.

He had seen him several times as the men worked and went out to do their personals. He assumed that was the purpose of the small building at the back of the compound. He had seen such things from a distance in Twin Springs. His brother wanted him to visit, but Chaska didn't trust the White men and disapproved of his men having free whiskey. He had seen what it did to other braves unaccustomed to drinking spirits. That was the only time he saw the one-armed man alone.

A wood fence surrounded the building, with a corral at the end and stables full of horses and mules. There were eight of each. That included the famous white stallion that yellow-hair rode. That was a prize Chaska wished for his own, but he knew he had to be crafty. All these mountain men were good shots and were knowl-edgeable of Indians' ways—and how they fought. He knew one of them lived with a Crow Indian. He had no idea how many enemies lived in their camp, but he meant to steer clear of them if possible. He rode with a sizable war party but couldn't stand up to a stronghold of warrior braves. They had to tread lightly and watch and listen carefully.

What Chaska planned to do was about who owned the land and who had the right to trap the streams and hunt the forests. This was what all the over thirty braves believed. Of course, no maps existed of what land belonged to which tribes, but they did know more or less where these boundaries lay. He knew a half day's walk past the cabins was a Crow camp. One of the mountain men lived there for part of the time. Now, he was in the house with his squaw. That made nine people in all. The Crow woman could be dangerous, too. They had to carefully assess the situation and their strengths and weaknesses before he finalized a plan.

Thirty warriors waited for War Chief Chaska, a few miles from the White men's cabins. They, too, were angry about the lack of furs and wild game to feed their families. When their children complained because they were hungry, the parents were forced to ride farther and take more risks to find enough food to survive. The larger tribes had many horses and could travel long distances to hunt, but theirs was small and poor in possessions, although they were big in spirit. They all wore war paint like their chief. It camouflaged them in the deep forest. Their arms and legs were covered in green and brown paint. It made them appear more dangerous. The whites of their eyes and their teeth flashed, revealing their position.

Forty broken-down horses grazed on the lush green summer grass. They were hobbled, and some stood on three legs, asleep. One blew and shook its head and clopped away. Others slid their jaws and flicked their tails at bottle flies. It was a hot day, and the animals were lethargic and moved sluggishly. The sound of buzzing flies filled the air, and it smelled of sweaty horses. They patiently waited until their war chief returned.

The warriors were impatient and anxious. They knew their opponents were strong and had excellent cover. They counted on Chaska to come up with an idea —a foolproof plan. He was the smartest of the tribe other than the chief, and even some doubted that. Tribal leaders, along with medicine men, often pumped up their images with stories of great victories from decades before. Chaska listened to such tales with little interest. Times had changed more with the Plains Indians in the last twenty years than they had during the previous ten thousand, all due to the encroachment of the White man on their land.

Most of these Sioux Indians had bows and arrows although a couple had rifles that they had traded for the few furs they had this season. A good gun was worth twelve to fourteen cold-weather pelts plus ammunition and powder. Chaska had decided that after the Rendezvous, they would have to rob the White men of their gold and silver. Then they could trade gold coins to buy everything their tribe needed to survive yet another harsh Rocky Mountain winter. They would rob them, vanquish them from their cabins, and kill the White man with yellow hair. Then they would burn their homes and eliminate every trace that they had ever been there.

Then, they would naturally inherit their strings of beaver traps all along Blackwater Creek as the spoils of war. They had seen many and heard there were four times what they had seen. His brother's friends had talked about the mountains of furs they sold that summer. Men like them didn't believe in White men's banks—they would have their money with them hidden somewhere. He saw he had several objectives; none could happen if all eight mountain men were still alive.

The woman didn't matter. She would return to her tribe even though the Crow men probably wouldn't want her after she had been with a White man. *It serves her right,* Chaska thought.

Beads of sweat rolled down his face, cutting tracks through the paint. A breeze rustled the leaves woven into his hair. From a distance, he looked like more trees and vegetation. He was a master at tracking and hiding. He knew he wasn't the warrior his brother was, but he was craftier. Chaska believed if he waited long enough, he would see what he was searching for: some break in their routine, or half the men leaving to hunt, making their numbers more manageable. If he were patient enough, something would appear or change, leaving him that small window of opportunity.

Sure, Chaska commanded more than thirty warriors, but he also knew his brother was the fiercest warrior in their tribe, and the White man with yellow hair had killed him. They both fought bravely, and his brother died with much honor. Still, Chaska felt he had been taken away from him, which was unfair. Now, his mother and father had changed in ways only parents who lose children do. He also knew they would never be the same again; he wouldn't, either.

Chaska spent the entire day under the hot summer sun. Still, he didn't move a finger. Hours passed as the glowing orb made its trajectory across the sky before nearing the western mountains. It slanted through the trees like rain. Now, the glare was in his eyes as he peered westward, leaving long shadows behind him. The sun appeared to hang on a string at the end of the world and threatened to disappear behind the mountains, allowing the night to capture it for another twelve hours.

Of course, he had heard of the mountain men that lived there. They had been living there for the last decade. Nobody had bothered them before. One reason was that there had always been enough wild game for everybody. The tribes had to travel farther to hunt to find enough to feed their families. The Sioux believed this land belonged to their tribe. Strangely enough, before now, nobody found it of any interest. That was why Mountain Dennis had been built there. He knew it didn't offend any neighboring Indians. As the game disappeared, the boundaries naturally broadened.

From the moment of contact, he knew it would be the survival of the fittest and bravest. Time seemed to stop and go. Moments felt like hours, and at other times, hours were like seconds. Chaska turned his eyes to his inner self, looking for the hint that would unlock the secret to destiny's plan. He had spoken to his tribe's medicine man before he left and was assured a sign would come to him if he were patient enough.

Chaska believed that soon there would be twenty lodges. Before, there were said to be six mountain men; now, there were eight or nine. Were the Sioux to allow them to make a village right there in the middle of the mountains? Three cabins were already an outrage. It had to be stopped. All these feelings he had against the White men were confusing. He knew he was told not to engage with yellow-hair, but he knew he must. It was only fair that they take their valuables.

They also had better horses than they did. Theirs were worn out and needed replacements. Chaska fancied the white stallion ridden by yellow-hair. He could see it all day, prancing nervously around the corral. It seemed like he was ready to break into a run at any moment. The horse was obviously high-spirited. Now, he was to see how high-spirited his owner was.

Every Indian in the mountains had heard of the games at the Rendezvous. They all heard about the ex-soldier beating the Sioux warrior. They even gave him a name. He was called Blade, which was all the Ute hunters had heard. They also knew that the old mountain man Rusty Steel lived there like he had been doing for many years. That, and now he had taken another man into his home. He was a sharpshooter named Levi Johnson. The Indians called him Beaver.

Chaska was quite aware of how dangerous these men were. The fact that they had built a small fortress was evident at first glance. He noted the gun slats on the windows' shutters. He spent the entire day sitting as still as a stone as he searched in his mind for a way to defeat the eight mountain men and take their traps and streams to keep for his tribe. Then there would be more wild game with them gone, too. He only had to figure out how to go about doing it.

Lightning bugs flashed in one place to be replaced by five more somewhere else. The yellow-green glow was visible in the dimming light. The sun slipped behind the Rocky Mountains, leaving a spectacle of colors like a prism.

It was time to leave. Chaska had spent two days

there and needed to return before his men thought something had happened to him. He hadn't eaten to reduce movement and could wait to tend to his personal needs. Few men could sit motionless for so long. He slipped his water bag over his shoulder and carefully backed out of the bushes. He continued to keep his eyes glued on the cabin. The windows lit up with kerosene lanterns, and the reflection of a fire flickered in the window like witches dancing. He knew the men must have powers. Now, he had to identify them to slow them down somehow. Time would not be on the Sioux's side.

He crawled through the bush as carefully as he could. If he broke a twig, one of the mountain men might hear. He was told they were like Indians in their ways; he just didn't know how much knowledge they had. That was yet to be determined. How could he render them defenseless before they approached? That would be his best option.

He knew he had men in his war party who had lost loved ones due to Indian raids. Some of them may not prove to be controllable by whoever was the chief of their small war party. He already knew who the strong-minded were and who the hardheaded were, too. He would have to keep a careful eye on the latter to ensure they didn't jump the gun.

The average Sioux warrior was not a patient man, so Chaska knew he had to give them something soon, or his power would begin to slip.

# MY RIGHT ARM

"YOU AIN'T HELPIN' HIM BY STAYING AT HIS SIDE SO YOU can help him do what he could before he lost his arm. Whatcha gonna do? Spend your whole life being his other hand?" Rusty Steel asked. "I've known many a man who lost a leg or an arm to a bear or ornery mountain lion, but that didn't mean they gave up doing everything they did before the loss. The sooner you let 'em tend to himself, the sooner he's gonna be back on his feet."

"Rusty's right, Levi," Blade said. "I had an officer who was missing one arm and an eye, and he still fought on the front line. Until he was killed, at least."

"But your arm ain't even healed yet," Levi replied. "We've gotta give ya a helping hand until the wound heals, at least."

"The longer you put it off, the harder it's gonna be," Rusty Steel said as he eyed the young soldier. "Having not had the experience, I can't say I know how ya feel, but I've had a pard or two that had the same happen, and they just went on about their way. Most folks living here in the wilderness make do with what they got and take their injuries and failures as lessons. It's all about seeing the glass half full or half empty, pilgrim. I prefer to see it half full all the time."

"Green Leaf said you're healin' just fine," Angus said. "As long as you put that cream on your stump like she showed ya, you won't get an infection."

"And how can you be so sure about that?" Blade Forrester asked.

"Why? Because it's Indian medicine!" Angus replied, shocked at what he considered a stupid question. "Any fool knows that. Ain't I right, Rusty?"

"Being as it's the only medicine we have up here other than castor oil and whiskey, it does the trick in a pinch," Rusty said.

"I've seen things White doctors couldn't cure, and medicine men could and did," Angus said, all matter of fact like. "Iffin you go to a city doctor, chances are you'll come out worse than when ya went in."

"And exactly what's that?" Rusty asked with mischief in his eyes. "What are these illnesses Indian medicine men can cure and a normal doctor can't?"

"I've never seen a White doctor cure the evil-eye or a black-cat curse, and medicine men do it all the time. I doubt there's a doctor in the country that can do that better than a Crow Indian shaman can."

Both Levi and Forrester were so puzzled it showed on their faces. They didn't know exactly what either one was. They weren't quite sure if they should laugh or take it seriously.

"Now I'm not sure what you're talkin' about," Levi ventured. "Black-cat curse?"

"Don't pay any attention to him, boys," Rusty said.

"Angus is more Indian than he is White man these days. It'll happens to some men when they spend a spell with the tribes."

"So far, that lotion is workin' just fine, Angus. I reckon Green Leaf is a fine nurse," Forrester said. "And, no offense intended, but I'd rather you not call me Blade anymore. It just don't fit me now. Just plain Bill will do fine."

"Well, Plain Bill it is." Rusty laughed. "You best think about what you ask for, son, because you might just get it."

Once they had a few cups of coffee after breakfast, they got to work. It was not only time to cure pelts and hides like always, it was also time to chop wood. The winters were long and cold, and you had to ensure you had enough. Now was the time to cut it so it would be dry when it came time to use.

This job usually befell the man on the bottom of the totem pole. That should have been Plain Bill, but since he lost his arm, it fell to Levi. With him standing six feet six inches tall and weighing in at over two hundred pounds, he went through the wood-cutting like a whittler making toothpicks. He chopped wood all day long like it was an easy chore. He could sling an axe one-handed and split a log as big as a fat man's leg. By the end of the day, they had a pile of firewood higher than a man's head.

Angus and his misses came out onto the porch at the end of the day, passed around tin cups, and poured each one full from a pitcher of cool lemonade. They sat around the porch and watched across the yard as the other two cabins' mountain men did the same. In the center of the yard was a place for a large campfire.

Sitting-sized logs were placed around it to make a triangle.

"What have we got to do tomorrow?" Levi asked.

"Why the same thing you did today. Tomorrow, the day after, and the day after that, you'll be cutting wood until you hate it, pilgrim. Angus and me keep curing the hides and beaver pelts. We've all got something to do. Unfortunately, you're workin' for both you and your friend, Plain Bill. Sorry about that, partner," Rusty said, "but that's how the game's played up here. Everybody has to pull their own load, and when one of us is laid up, the next man under him, or in this case above him, takes up the slack."

"Don't you worry, none," Rusty said. "The boys across the way have been up to the same things as we have. Lookee over there. Here comes Mountain Dennis right now."

"It's been a hot one today," Dennis said as he stared at the pile of firewood. "How about you come over to my place and cut some of those trees up for me?" The last light of the day flashed off his gold front teeth.

"I'll be glad to help ya as soon as I finish my chores." Levi smiled.

"Who said you were ever gonna be done with your chores?" Rusty chuckled. "Don't worry, son. I won't let you sit on your backside around here. We've always got something that needs to be done."

"When we goin' huntin'?" Levi asked. Then he remembered Bill, who was sitting beside him. "Do you think you can still shoot a rifle?"

"I intend to do everything I did before I lost my arm, and some things even better," Bill Forrester said. "I believe it will be a matter of practice and repetition. I'm not saying it will be easy or fast, but I have to believe I can hold my own again. If not, I suppose I'll have to climb down the mountain, which is not exactly an option for me now."

"Atta boy, Bill," Levi said. "I knew if anybody had it in 'em, it would be you, pard."

Mountain Dennis twitched his nose several times, then rubbed it and sniffed the air. He wrinkled his nose and said, "I've got an inkling we've got company."

Levi gave a three-sixty and didn't see anybody. "Whatcha mean? I don't see another living soul but us who live here."

"Just because you don't see something doesn't mean it ain't there," Dennis said. He sniffed the air again. "I know none of us use bear grease to cover our skin. I do know of some warriors that do just that. It keeps 'em warm at night and during the winter months. Has anybody ever told ya not to wash with White man's soap in the wilderness because the Indians can smell it?"

"Yeah, I've heard that and even seen it," Levi replied.

"Iffin you develop a fine nose for bear fat, you ward off a few surprises by the local hostiles," Dennis said. His eyes scoured the brush and woods, but it was so thick, you couldn't see more than twenty feet past the yard and into the forest.

Levi followed his gaze until Rusty said, "Stop being so obvious, young man. You don't want the Indian to know we're aware he's there. He thinks he's gonna surprise us, and now we've gotta make up a little surprise for him. I doubt he be alone, either. It would be foolish of a warrior to traipse around this part of the mountains all on his lonesome."

"I doubt there's one, but I only catch a faint smell.

Iffin it's more, it won't be more than two. Any more, and we'd see 'em."

Levi Johnson couldn't resist looking, but he did so as inconspicuously as possible. But no matter how hard he strained his eyes, all he could see were green branches, bushes, brambles, and brown tree trunks. He smelled the air, but all he smelled was pine trees and the coffee they sipped on.

"What do you think they're up to?" Forrester asked. "From what I've seen, where there's one or two Indians, there's a considerable force behind them."

"You're smarter than you look." Dennis grinned. "The question is, what we are gonna do about it? One thing they'll be after for sure are the horses. Especially with that white stallion of yours, Plain Bill." He laughed good-heartedly.

"It's that or the kin of the Sioux Indian the captain killed," Rusty said, now serious. "Maybe they ain't gonna let cha forget who you are, son."

"I thought it was a big deal for a warrior to die an honorable death," Levi said.

"You've been readin' too many nickel novels, boy," Dennis said. "All that's in 'em is tales and lies. How would you feel if some intruder came to your home and killed your father or your brother?"

"I reckon I'd feel pretty bad," Levi replied. "Maybe enough to wanna get even."

"You might not like it, but there it is in a nutshell. Life up here is hard for the strongest of men. Now with one arm, I reckon you best learn all you can with one hand because one way or another, we got company, and I doubt they be friendly."

"That's crazy talk," Levi said. "Bill can't do anything

yet. He only lost his arm a couple or three weeks ago. He needs months to recuperate."

"I'm sorry, son, but he don't have months," Dennis said. "He's gonna have to stand up and defend himself like all of us, or he might end up dead anyway."

"It's a good thing Green Leaf left ahead of me and went back to the Crow camp," Angus said. "I know the fellas out there ain't Crow, or we would have already been warned. I reckon Dennis is right, and they be Sioux and are here for vengeance. Or it could be Ute or Blackfeet saying we be on their land."

"When I came here, nobody wanted to live or hunt here because it was so isolated," Dennis said. "That was just what I wanted back then. Nowadays, it don't seem so far away from other folks. Maybe with the hunting scarcer, they might be offended we're huntin' their elk and trappin' their beaver."

"Whoever they are, I don't reckon we'll have to wait for long until they show themselves," Rusty said. "Iffin they know anything about us, they'll know we can shoot the eyeballs off a dragonfly, so they have somethin' up their sleeve."

"How can you be so sure somebody's out there if you haven't seen 'em?" Levi asked.

"Because we've been livin' up here for over a decade, and we know when somethin' ain't right," Rusty said. "With time, you'll have the instinct, too. Dennis smells it, but I feel it now in my gut. We've got company, all right. It's just a matter of time before they make a move."

"And how long is that gonna be?" Levi asked.

"It all depends on whether they're a bunch of hunters or real warrior braves," Rusty replied. "Iffin they're the latter, they'll be here to fight and not just steal the horses."

"So, what do we do about it?" Forrester asked. "Every encounter we've had with Indians has been a disaster."

"Yeah, but they were Comanche," Angus said. "They be a special breed of their own. Nobody fights like a Comanche warrior. These most likely be Blackfeet or Ute iffin they're after the horses, but iffin they're after the captain, they'll be Sioux."

"Which is worse, a Blackfoot or a Sioux?" Levi asked.

"Which is more dangerous," Rusty asked, "a rifle or a pistol? Both of 'em will kill ya dead."

# MOUNTAIN MEN

NIGHT HAD FALLEN, AND THE CINDERS FROM PIPES, cheroots, and cigarettes glowed orange in the dark. A metal kerosene lantern sat on the porch table with the wick turned down. It cast sufficient yellow light to see and not fall but not enough for someone in the dark to take a potshot at a member of their family. Most of these six men had spent so much time together that they felt more like brothers than simple friends. Even though they knew the threat was there, they didn't seem nervous or conspicuous while preparing for a battle if that was in the cards for today.

Even Levi was being pushed along and accepted due to his natural wilderness skills. The same couldn't be said for his friend, ex-Captain Bill Forrester. What was once a brave officer was a different man with one arm. Now, Syracuse Sam, Portland Pete, and Yosemite Bob had joined the rest of the neighbors. As soon as it got dark, everyone armed themselves to the teeth. Some men had four flintlock pistols in their belts. They kept their weapons covered with their buckskin shirts and rifles in the shadow of the porch. It was going to be a long night.

Levi Johnson and Bill Forrester had their Hawken rifles primed and loaded, and each wore a brace of pistols. They felt strange because they were waiting for something they hadn't seen, heard, or smelled. It was like they were awaiting a figment of somebody's imagination, and at the same time, they knew it was probably as accurate as everything else they had encountered so far. Even normal everyday life was a challenge and dangerous in the wilderness.

Levi briefly wondered if he would be left behind in the Rocky Mountains and buried in an unmarked grave like most. Just then, he felt like he was a million miles away from southwestern Indiana. Right then, he felt so far away that something told him he would never return to see his folks again.

Until then, almost every encounter Levi Johnson had had with Indians had been hostile. If they were out there, he didn't doubt that these, too, were his soon-to-be enemy, whom he might have to kill for him to survive. Despite the cool mountain air, rivulets of sweat ran down Levi's back, pooling in his shirt. He wiped his face dry with his bandana. Most of his encounters had come with the Army as protection, although that proved insufficient. The rest had happened by surprise, or at least unexpectedly.

When they attacked the Comanche for burning the small wagon train and the people with it, they had gone with the intention of killing, and killing was what they did. When the Indians attacked them on the trail, they intended to kill all the White men and nearly succeeded. Now, there were fewer than ever. Even though the other men confirmed the looming attack, they didn't seem as bothered as Levi or the captain.

"How long do ya think they'll wait before they come at us?" Levi whispered.

Rusty Steel harrumphed and looked at the young mountain man. "One day, you'll look back on that question and think how stupid it was. First of all, iffin they ain't here yet, we best enjoy the quiet. It could be a long wait. They could try to starve us out."

"But there's plenty of game," Forrester said before he realized how stupid it was. It would be too dangerous to go out and hunt with the Sioux watching. They still didn't know how many were there, but one or two for sure, according to Mountain Dennis. They expected there to be more not far away, though. The six mountain men had suffered countless attacks on their cabins—primarily after they built buildings two and three. No one seemed to mind Dennis's presence when he was alone. When more cabins were added, the local Indians viewed them more as a threat. If they built three buildings, how many would there be in five years?

"I bet I could sneak past whoever's out there," Levi said, full of youthful confidence. He blurted it out before even thinking about what he said.

"Did I just hear you volunteer to go out there all on your lonesome to hunt us some fresh meat?" Rusty said. "Boy-o-boy, are you the feisty one. You must have ice-cold water running through your veins, young man. We'll wait here and build a fire for when you come back with a big buck elk."

"I reckon I can sneak out and be back before dawn," Levi said. "I don't wanna shoot nothin', or I'll let the

Indians know where I am. I'll have to make some traps, but just the same, I ain't chicken."

"Atta boy, I reckon that's the spirit," Rusty said. "If you're willin', I might just go with ya for the thrill." It was clear to the other mountain men Rusty Steel was just making fun and hacking on one of the new men. Apparently, Levi didn't know it and thought he was serious.

"Don't listen to that old fart," Portland Pete said. "He'll get ya scalped just for a little entertainment. You do know he used to be a pirate, don't ya?"

"Don't listen to all that rubbish Pete tells ya," Rusty spat. "I was a captain on my own paddle boat. That part is true enough, but I was never a pirate. To my dismay, I lost my vessel to French pirates, which was a heck of an embarrassment. My first mate was shot and killed. The Frenchies were smuggling guns on my boat. They hid them in crates that were supposed to be full of steel traps. In the end, I was the one that got trapped. I grew up in the streets of St. Louis as an orphan. My old captain threw me in the drink for trying to steal a purse, and I nearly drowned. He fished me out and gave me a job. I spent most of my life aboard a river-faring vessel, although I've navigated the open seas, too."

"How about we get to matters more urgent than you two tellin' lies to these two fine young men?" Syracuse Sam chuckled. He was the oldest of the bunch, with white hair and a drooping handlebar mustache. He thought the growth on his lip made him look taller, but somehow, it made him appear smaller.

"How long before they hit us, you're askin'?" Rusty said, enunciating every syllable to ensure the two young men understood. "It could be at twelve noon. But then again, they usually hit at night—either dusk or dawn. If they came at us in the middle of the day, there would be no surprise. Whoever they are, I doubt they be stupid. We need to figure out what kind of schemes they've got up their sleeve before they get a chance to set their trap. That'll be the trick to this one. So, the longer the Indians take to figure out what they wanna do, the longer we have to figure it out for ourselves and prepare accordingly."

"The truth is, youngins, they may take a night, or they might take two weeks," Angus said as he eyed the edge of the forest. "It all depends on how many braves the war party leader can lose and still save face. He thinks we're wicked hard and smart, so he'll be biding his time. We've gotta take for granted they have eyes on us at all times. So don't go out to do your business unless you've got two men with ya. And it's best iffin y'all do it at night, so it's harder to see us and get an arrow or a shot off."

"That's right," Sam said. "Iffin ya gotta take a leak, it's best ya do it here inside the compound behind the cabin. If one of us has to go to the outhouse, two of us will stand guard outside the door with our guns ready. At night, it'll be difficult for them to see how well-armed we are. I'm thinkin' like Rusty here and believe it may be Sioux lookin' to get even for the death of that Sioux warrior that got his head lopped off by Plain Bill."

"I still say I can sneak out of camp and find out where the Indians are and pick us up something fresh to eat. I ain't afraid as long as I'm on my own," Levi said, full of confidence. "Back in the woods in Indiana, I tracked many men and animals, and none of 'em have ever seen me. Not before I shot nor after, because I never miss."

"So you think you can sneak out of here and spy on those Indians, do ya?" Rusty said. Now he wasn't laughing. "I've seen more experienced men than you try to do such a thing and fail."

"I said I could sneak up on 'em—I never said I could tackle 'em by myself," Levi replied. "If they're here in the forest and ain't headed back to their tribe, they're mine."

"Don't we need a signal or something?" Rusty snickered. "You know, for when the hostiles catch ya, and we've got to come and rescue ya from the Indians." He laughed like it was all a game to him.

"No need to, brother," Levi said, smiling. "I'll find out their strength and weaknesses. Then we can discuss what we might do to stop 'em. Maybe we can find a friendly way to do this."

"Now he's turned into our ambassador for the Indians." Rusty laughed until he got a stitch. "He's gonna teach us a thing or two after all these years in the mountains. You've got to stop, boy. You're gonna give me a stroke from laughing."

As the mountain men chuckled at the boldness of the young pathfinder, Levi stepped to the edge of the porch and the faint curtain of light that circled the table. That was when it hit them. He was as serious as death about heading out into the woods with Sioux Indians or something as bad spying on them. At least that was what Dennis swore and smelled, and he was rarely wrong about Indians. He had lived in the mountain the longest and had learned the Indian ways better than most.

"I'll be back in a spell," Levi whispered as he stepped into the dark and instantly disappeared.

Rusty opened his mouth to tell the young man he was joking, but it was too late. He vanished like smoke through a keyhole. The aging mountain man sat with his mouth open and his chin on his chest.

"Where'd he go?" Rusty asked.

"Now you've gone and done it," Dennis spat. "You know there's a good chance that youngster ain't gonna come back, don't cha?"

"Dagnabit, I never expected him to have the grit to take me seriously. He went and ran off before I could tell him I was only joshin'," Rusty said. He was shocked. He was just having fun with the new member of their group, and the young fellow took him seriously.

"Now we're gonna have to wait to see what happens next," Dennis said, angry. "Once first light comes, we best go out and try to find 'em before the Sioux or whoever the heck is out there waiting on us. Hopefully, I was wrong and smelled something else."

"You ain't ever been wrong as long as I've known ya," Rusty said. "I doubt you'll start to make mistakes today."

Captain Bill Forrester felt worse than ever. Now his best friend, whom he'd taken as his partner, had disappeared into the night after more Indians. Bill wished he could have gone with him but was still weak from losing this arm. He knew half of his problem was in his head. He had to push the trauma aside and pull himself together quickly. There wasn't time to continue to wallow in self-pity. He had to confront the loss and somehow overcome it and become a better mountain man because of it. He knew he had it in him. He had graduated from West Point, so he had the smarts.

Forrester hadn't shown it outwardly. He had it hidden inside like he usually did, but until more Indians showed up, he hadn't been trying as hard as he could have. All that was time lost, and he didn't intend to be left behind due to his injury. He began to practice raising his rifle with one arm. It was challenging to keep the barrel steady with such a heavy weapon. Lucky for him, he had always been as good a shot with a pistol with one hand as the other; the same with using his saber. At West Point, he was so skilled with his right hand, sometimes he offered competitions with his left hand to make it more interesting.

Levi's Army buddy sat brooding at the edge of the porch. He practiced throwing his knife into the post with his left hand. Something told him that despite his injuries, he would be drawn into the fray when the time came. He intended to be as prepared as he could. When he was done, he began to sharpen his saber. He had to shrug off the fact that he had lost an arm and show he had the backbone to do this. Next, he would clean his guns. He didn't want to be shooting blanks if things went south.

Now he decided he was the one who had to think up a plan to defend the cabins against attack. That and get Levi out of trouble if he got caught by the Indians in the dark of night. He was trained in tactical warfare and had all the smarts needed to solve the problem at hand. Still, it lurked in his mind that all this assumption was due to a man saying he smelled an Indian. It began to seem far-fetched to the captain more all the time, but now Levi had wandered out into the night alone, which was always dangerous in the wilderness.

As soon as Levi stepped into the dark of night, he

how that smelled anyway. He was looking for something different. What he smelled was ordinary coffee. He was so surprised he was put off his feed for a moment. Then he carefully took a half dozen more steps and smelled sizzling meat. He suddenly realized he had found their camp. Now, he had to be more careful than ever. Surely, they had a night guard out, if not more. Levi still didn't know how many Indians would be there. Of course, he had seen Indians drink and buy coffee at the Rendezvous. That, and plenty of tobacco. It appeared they shared a liking of both with the White men.

Levi got onto his belly and, with his Hawken cradled in his arms, crawled toward the smell. Now he began to hear whispers. He pushed his head into a thick, green bush and spread the branches apart slightly so he could peek through with one eye. He moved like a sloth, he was so slow. His movements were very deliberate, and he never made a sound, not even the rustling of the leaves on the bush he hid behind.

# SIOUX WARRIORS

LEVI JOHNSON CLOSED ONE EYE AND USED HIS HANDS TO separate the brush before him. The only thing visible was one white eye. He stifled a gasp when he saw how many dark men squatted before a small fire. They each had a chunk of meat in their hands, tearing at it with their teeth. Levi's belly grumbled. He held his breath. He was sure they must have heard it but apparently not. He counted thirty-three warriors. They wore buckskin shirts, breechcloths, and leggings with moccasins, and they were all armed.

Each man had bows and arrows, and two had long rifles. A year ago, Levi would have thought bows and arrows weren't a match for pistols and rifles, but he had learned differently. He was both shocked and surprised when he saw how fast the Comanche shot arrows at them. They could shoot twenty arrows in a minute and throw a lance so far it seemed impossible. Their horsemanship was unrivaled worldwide. He had never seen such people prepared for their peculiar way of life.

Levi had no idea how good the Sioux were with

their weapons, but he doubted they were shabby. All these warrior tribes had survived thousands of years. He imagined that even if they weren't up to scratch with the Comanche, he doubted they'd be a piece of cake. He was still shocked at how many there were. There were more braves than when they were attacked on the trail to Colorado, where they lost so many men the expedition was abandoned.

Still, Levi couldn't tell if they were warriors or hunters until he clearly caught sight of one of them. The orange glow of the fire illuminated his face. He was covered in warpaint shades of green and looked like the plants surrounding him. Their bodies were painted, too. One of the warriors had leaves braided into his hair. Something told Levi that was the man who was spying on them. He noted they dressed like the Sioux warrior Forrester killed. Dennis had been right after all.

Levi watched for a while but couldn't understand what they said. After taking mental notes of everything he saw, he slowly backed out of his blind. He crawled fifty yards before he crouched into a run to put some distance between the Sioux and him and carefully swung around to the other side of their campsite. He still didn't see the guard, but he knew there must be one there. Whether the Indian guard had seen him or not remained to be seen. All he knew was that they were in a world of trouble if that bunch got after them.

He got far enough away that he wouldn't be heard, and he began to huff and puff with the heels of his hands on his knees as his heart hammered between his ears. He was worn out, more from the tension than the physical exercise. He carefully moved around the camp to the other side and found their horses. That was when he saw the single guard. He had a jug of liquor in his hand.

He must have brought it from the Rendezvous. The Indian looked around suspiciously and took a long swig as his Adam's apple bobbed up and down. Then he quickly hid the jug under a blanket. Levi waited for a while, and as he expected, the guard got woozy from the moonshine and began to doze off. Levi wondered if his chief knew he was drinking on guard duty.

Levi moved carefully into the roped-off pen they had made for the horses. He made a rough count and found there were more than forty. He knew he had to unhobble them as quickly as he could. All he needed was for one horse to squeal from fright, and he would arouse suspicion, and over thirty Sioux would be after him. His razor-sharp knife sliced through the ropes like they were whipped cream. He made short work of a long job as he cut the bindings hobbling their front legs.

Then Levi deftly leaped onto the back of a big mustang and slowly walked it out of the field. He pulled up and waited until several other horses became curious and followed. Soon thirty of the horses were walking deeper into the forest; the rest slowly followed. Levi didn't know the area very well yet, but he knew where he had been and had his bearings straight.

As soon as they were far enough away, he brought the mustang into a trot, and the others followed. He led them several miles in the opposite direction toward the big Crow camp. Hopefully, the Crow Indians where Angus's wife lived would find them before the Sioux. It would be perilous for them to come so close to a Crow stronghold. At least he had put them afoot, leaving them with less advantage.

Finally, Levi jumped down and slapped the mustang on the rump, and he shot off like a bullet with the rest of the herd behind him. They ran even closer to the camp full of Crow Indians. Now, the young mountain man turned, and his heart redlined as he raced toward the cabins and to safety. He believed he knew where all the Sioux warriors were, so he abandoned much of his caution. He didn't want to return to the cabins after daylight. He might get himself shot for his effort if the Sioux were a step or two ahead of him.

Leaves and small branches slapped his skin as he raced through the forest. Blood speckled his shirt as the branches scratched and cut at his face and arms. Occasionally, he could see the sun overhead, and he would correct his bearings slightly and run faster. His fists pumped up and down like a steam engine as Levi ran for his life. He knew the whole war party would be after him as soon as the horses were found missing.

He slid to a stop and peeked into the next clearing. All three traps were full. He smiled and gathered his catch, and now he was almost home, so he trotted the rest of the way. His heart slowed, and he caught his rhythm now that he didn't have to run holus-bolus for his life.

When he burst into the clearing of the compound, he found himself with a half dozen barrels pointed his way. It was still dark, but all the mountain men immediately recognized Levi's massive silhouette.

"Wait, don't shoot. It's me, boys, and I brought fresh turkey, too." Levi grinned so wide you could see his tonsils. He held up three plump birds in his fist.

"Well, I'll be danged," Dennis said. "Your young friend appears to have pulled it off. We'll have turkey for dinner tonight. There ain't nothin' like a well-cooked bird with potatoes and gravy."

"The next time you run off like that, I'm gonna knock you out before you step off the porch," Rusty growled. "You should know better than to believe what I say. I'm always joking and hackin' on the boys, but that don't mean I really want cha to do it. Then again, I'll be danged if ya didn't."

"Don't hack on me for doin' what I'm told to do," Levi retorted. "If ya don't want me to do something, don't tell me to do it. I thought you was smarter than that, Rusty."

"The only one that thinks Rusty is as smart as he is, is Rusty Steel." Dennis laughed.

"So, did ya see the Indians?" Angus asked.

"I'm afraid I did. I got lucky, and the fella guarding the horses was nippin' on a jug of corn whiskey, and I caught 'im drunk and half asleep. I got a count of the Indians, and there were thirty-three. They had forty horses, but I run 'em off, so now they're on foot."

"You ran their horses off?" Dennis asked with apparent shock. "All by yourself? Where'd ya run 'em off to?"

"Toward the Crow camp where Green Leaves lives. I figured if they kept running, soon they'd run into some of your wife's kin, Angus. That way, the Sioux are set afoot, and your folks have more horses. Now they have one less advantage."

The mountain men broke out laughing. They could hardly believe what they were hearing. The big young man was as good as his word and could track as good as any man present, bar none.

"But weren't they hobbled or nothing?" Sam asked. "Usually, they make a rope pen and hobble 'em all."

"Yes, sir, they were, but I cut the rope with my knife. It's double-edged, so when one side gets dull, I still have the other blade."

"Well, I'll be." Rusty smiled. Despite the confusion he created by making fun of the boy, he turned out to be as capable as any of them.

He was proud he had brought Levi Johnson to his cabin in the mountains. It looked like he had a future in the trapping business. They even had turkey for dinner.

Levi looked around the porch and saw Bill sitting on the edge with his legs dangling over the side. He was listening to everything, but his mouth was no more than a gash. He noticed his jaw as he ground his teeth.

"You should have been there with me, pard," Levi said. "These Indians were even scarier than the Comanche, although I don't know how fierce they really be. I snuck up close enough to have a peek and ran for the hills."

"Yeah, after ya ran off their horses." Dennis laughed. "You are quite the mountain man already, ain't cha, son?"

Levi heard what Dennis said despite the laughter, and it filled him with pride. If a mountain man of his caliber said he was an equal, no doubt he was.

"What else can ya tell us about the Indians?" Dennis asked. "How did they dress? How well were they armed?"

"They dressed just like the Sioux warrior that Bill Forrester here killed. They were all painted up for war, too. The only weakness I saw in them was one of 'em was drinkin' whiskey. I don't know if the war chief knows about it or not. With any luck, we'll have a few of 'em drunk if they bought whiskey at the Rendezvous and have it hidden from their chief. I don't see a Sioux leader letting his night guards get drunk on the job."

"That's food for thought," Dennis replied. "If they're over thirty, there's no way they'll be heading back home before they come and give us a visit, regardless of whether a few are drunk or not."

"I've been thinking about how we can defend the cabins," Forrester said. "I'm not saying I know more than you men about it all, but I went to West Point, and we studied war tactics that may help us here against these Sioux that I've brought down on you all and I'm sorry for that. Ever since we headed west, I've had a hard time. I've even lost an arm. Maybe I can make it up with some ideas about protecting the houses and the stables."

"That's foolish talk," Levi said. "What happened back at the Rendezvous was just a game. The Sioux warrior was who was out of line here. He had no call to take something won fair and square and turn it into a grudge. Men like that shouldn't be allowed to compete. Why is it the White man and Indians can't get along?"

"Ain't it obvious?" Rusty asked. "We're all guilty. There are so many White folks they outnumber the Indians ten to one and with modern weapons, too. Soon, it'll be a hundred to one. You just wait and see. We've already killed off more than half the buffalo, and elk get harder to bag each season. It's the same with the beaver. Sure, it seems like we still do all right, but we were trapping twice as many ten years ago. We're slowly taking land, food, and shelter that's belonged to them for as far back as anyone can remember. Now, the country is full of Europeans and Americans and more and more and comin' every day."

"What is this you say about preparing the cabins for when the Sioux come and attack us?" Dennis asked. "Usually, we just batten down and let 'em try to get at us. That's why we built the cabins so sturdy. I'm all ears if you've got any ideas after what Levi here did. You boys don't seem as green as we thought you were."

"Battening down the shutters and bracing the door doesn't sound like much of a plan," Forrester said. "I studied what was called guerrilla warfare. It was used in Europe in warfare in some cases and was effective. Maybe we can make a twist or two to the theory and get it to work for us."

"Maybe bringing these two young rascals up here with us this year was a good move." Portland Pete chuckled. "I wasn't too keen on the idea at first, but it looks like we might have needed some young blood in the group before we all die off or get kilt by bears or hostiles."

"We ain't lost none of us six yet in the last ten years or so," Angus said. "I doubt they'll kill us this time, either. They've been at it long enough you'd think they would all agree to give it up. All they do is get their men killed or wounded. Unless they got something new, I doubt they get past the post fence."

Plain Bill Forrester had lost his pride on the trail from Wichita and his arm in the Rocky Mountains. He wondered what he was going to lose next. All he had left were his stones and his word, and he hoped he didn't break either one with what he was planning. He was as pleased as punch about his buddy's success, but now he had to prove he was worth having around, too, or he would be just another mouth to feed.

If he could devise a defensive plan to catch the Indians off guard when they did attack, he might be able to turn this around and scare them off. Bill knew he had to plan carefully because his reputation was at stake. He was aware he was partly responsible for the Sioux warriors being there in the first place. They didn't just happen upon them, that was for sure. If Forrester could do his part to impress these men, they might respect him like they did his friend Johnson.

# WHITE MEN

WHEN THE ALARM WAS CALLED AND CHASKA FOUND OUT their horses had been spirited off in the night, he first suspected Blackfeet or Ute Indians. He didn't think the Crow would come that far from their camp. When the war chief discovered his guard was drunk, he was furious.

"You know I told you I don't allow my men to go to the Rendezvous, but you had to go anyway, didn't you?" Chaska spat. "And this fool brought White man's poison with him and lost our horses. How many of you have whiskey? I know Dark Horse isn't the only one who brought a jug. Do I have to look in every man's things, or are you going to be men and fess up?"

Seven braves stood, including Dark Horse, with ceramic jugs hanging from their fingers. They could barely stand. They wobbled from side to side. The man nearest War Chief Chaska suddenly burped. It wasn't intentional and just slipped out, but the culprit was humiliated just the same. The whole war party was embarrassed to a certain degree. But then again, most of them felt that Chaska was too harsh a leader. He always made them train or go on more war parties than the other groups of braves. They didn't complain because he never asked them to do something he wouldn't and was always the first one into battle when the occasion arose. Still, he was so disciplined himself, he expected nothing less of his other warriors.

Now, War Chief Chaska had more than a quarter of his men drunk and all his horses missing, and he was so angry smoke was coming out of his ears. Those sober knew better than to say a word or the wrath of their chief man fall on them.

The warrior who burped said, "Let's go kill the White men." Then he turned and spewed up his meal. When he finished, he staggered three feet and fell flat on his face.

He was as useless as the other six braves. None of them were accustomed to drinking, and it didn't sit well with them at all. The chief was furious and getting madder by the minute.

"All seven of you get out of my sight right now!" Chaska roared. "You are to return to our camp, but I want to see broken bottles before you do. There will be no White man's whiskey in my war party. You all have shamed yourselves."

The drunken Indians reluctantly threw their moonshine jugs to the ground, watching them shatter. A tear streaked one Indian's cheek. He could barely stand on his own.

"Before you go, all seven of you are to get after our horses," Chaska barked. "When you find them, bring them back here. You are to return home on foot. Without our horses, my plan won't work, fools. You don't deserve the honor of riding a warrior's horse. All seven of you are demoted to hunters again, which isn't negotiable. I won't have one of my warrior's drinking White man's poison."

The seven braves turned to follow the tracks of the stolen horses. They staggered from one side of the trail to the other, such was their depth of inebriation. With forty animals, there was no secret about their direction. A blind man could follow the tracks.

The chief yelled, "And don't you dare come back to my camp without our animals! If you don't locate them, then find another Sioux camp to live in. You're not welcome in mine unless you succeed. Act like your lives depend on your results. That might very well be the case."

Chaska was beside himself. He had been so careful in the days before, suffering the heat and lack of food, only to have someone steal their horses. He figured it had to be Crow Indians because no White man could sneak up on a Sioux war party. They had seen how the rope used to hobble the horses had been cut. What puzzled the war chief was why and how only one Indian brave came to steal their horses when they would usually bring enough men to control the herd. But they saw only the one man's tracks.

It just didn't make any sense, although it didn't change the fact that they were set afoot, and there was nowhere around that was safe to steal or trade for more horses. They were in a sort of no man's land for all the tribes. Before, nobody had been interested in Black-water Creek because it was small and out of the way. Rarely did Indians from any tribe come to this small and relatively insignificant valley. They all knew White men lived there, though. Every Indian on the mountain knew this. That was precisely why the White men had chosen such a place to live.

Chaska had heard more than a decade before that a White man named Mountain Dennis Breed had arrived. He brought steel tools, knives, and beautiful beads to trade with the Indians, and nobody seemed to mind his presence despite his trespassing. A few years later, they heard in the Indian gossip that four more men had come to live in the distant valley and had built two more cabins. Initially, he was alone, so over the years, some people forgot he was even there.

Once more White men joined him, they considered it trespassing. By then, they had had encounters with other White men, and those were violent. Their opinion of these intruders had changed from innocent, friendly people to White men who wanted to steal their land, game, and shelter. Most Plains Indians used buffalo for nearly everything, from coats and capes to meat, and from hide to make their teepees to bones to make fishing hooks and sewing needles.

The war chief knew that if he were to lead a war party into the wilderness to evict the White men and burn their homes to the ground, he would be in the songs of his elders. At forty years old, he knew he didn't have much time before his chance would pass, and he would be too old to leave a legend behind. By leaving a legend, he would live in the future even after he had passed on to the spirit world.

*Calm down before you make a fool of yourself,* Chaska chided himself. He would only make it worse by overreacting to something that was becoming more and more common. When they returned with the horses, they might have more information on what actually happened. Obviously, a single warrior had broken their lines like they weren't there and ridden off on their animals without waking anybody. He still didn't know how one man could have pulled this off.

"All of you, calm down right now," Chaska growled. When he was angry, his voice sounded like a wild animal. "The next man I catch drunk, I'm going to hang them by their feet while I skin them for their sins. All the plans we had included using our horses. Now, we must change all our plans because I doubt those fools who got drunk will ever find them. They will be too close to the Crow camp, and they won't be as brave as the warrior that took them from us in the first place."

"What do we do now?" Black Mink asked.

"I think we better go to the edge of their compound to set siege. First, we'll stop them from coming and going," Chaska said. "That will give us time to figure out what to do next. I'll come up with something. I always do."

"How long do you think they will hold out?" Black Mink asked. "You know we aren't the first Indians that tried to force them to leave. All the others have lost warriors to their rifles and failed. We better tread with caution, Chaska. We don't want to leave a disaster as our legacy."

"What do I look like, a medicine man? Your guess is as good as mine. I've heard they're a scrappy bunch, but I've never seen a White man fight better than an Indian," Chaska said. "Our main danger will be their guns, and the hunters usually have the best. Once we kill them, we can steal their weapons and gold and claim their beaver traps are ours. Nobody will dispute our claim, not this close to our camp and with all the White men dead. Maybe we will even move our small tribe here if the chief agrees. This is our moment to bask in glory, old friend. If we let this pass, we may never have another chance."

"But we *have* seen White men fight better than Indians," Black Mink said. "All fear that mountain man who killed your brother with the saber. Maybe these people trespassing on Indian property are more skilled than we are. Not all of them but at least a few."

"Without horses, it will be more difficult to move fast and attack at night like we planned. Now, instead of rushing them with horses before they know we're there, we'll have to do it on foot. We will carry on forward no matter what," Chaska said. "I have never returned from a raiding party as the loser rather than the victor, and I don't intend to start now. There are only eight of them, and we are thirty-three."

"We were thirty-three but now are twenty-six. You have sent seven warriors home for drinking whiskey. What exactly does *no matter what* mean?" Black Mink asked. "Are we to throw all caution aside, or are we going to rethink your old plan and come up with a new one?"

Chaska nodded as he listened and thought. They still had the element of surprise, but they wouldn't have the speed they would on horseback, so rushing the cabins was out of the question. They could have reached the White men with their horses before they had time to batten down the shutters and grab their weapons. He had planned to ride his spotted mustang into the front door of the first cabin he came to and slay the White men present. Now, they would have to be patient and set siege on the compound to ensure they didn't get food or get in or out.

It was too bad it wasn't cold out, or they would also have to come out to gather firewood. They would still have to cook what food they had. Chaska knew that during the summer months, there was sufficient game, and they didn't have large stores of food like they did during the winter. Now, they would go out every few days to kill fresh meat. After a long winter, nobody wanted to eat salted bears or elk anymore. Freshly killed wild game tasted so much better.

Chaska had heard from a wise elder that each man had ten days to claim his fortune. Ten in all, if your life depended on it. Looking back through the lens of time, he hoped he would stand apart from the rest. Of course, he was ready to die for what he felt was right. That, and the opportunity to leave a legacy before so many White men came to their land; they would no longer own anything. For him, all the rest was dust and clutter and had no purpose in his new life.

He intended to become a famous war warrior. Maybe one day he would become chief himself. That is, if he survived, but to him, that was less important than his legacy. He had watched his father and his father's father pass to the spirit world, and they were no longer mentioned in the stories at night because they left no legacy. He didn't intend to make the same mistake.

It had been an hour since first light, and the sun was already climbing into the sky, making the men sweat. They silently gathered their weapons and turned to follow their war chief, Chaska. They all knew the original plan they had agreed to had been eliminated. Some of them had only agreed because their leader had a good plan. They all knew these mountain men had been attacked on a dozen occasions over the decade, and they weren't the first. They intended to succeed where all others failed. Chaska didn't know it, but there was discontent among his ranks. But the men were too afraid of him to voice their opinions. They knew that whatever they said at this point would fall on deaf ears.

He started at a trot toward where he had seen the White men in their houses. With twenty-five men, he knew he could keep them in their cabins, but now he had to think of a way to kill them inside their shelter or force them out. His original plan was general Indian war tactics, but starving people held at a siege wasn't the best solution for Indian war parties.

Most of the men volunteered because they were pumped up to kill White men, but when they had to wait for long periods, they would lose their focus and eventually their interest. Many war parties were held together by a thread and a promise. Now Chaska couldn't promise anybody anything other than the fight that appeared to be inevitable.

Now, the odds would be too equal for the war chief's taste, but what was he to do? Would they be aware they were there and be waiting for them? He racked his brain for an idea of how he could breach their fences and reach the front door before they were cut down with the mountain men's rifles.

# PLAIN BILL'S PLAN

"SO WHAT IS THIS PLAN YOU WERE TELLING US ABOUT, young man?" Rusty Steel asked, now more interested in what the two newcomers had to say.

Levi's initiative had changed how Rusty looked at the two young men. They had made it across Kansas when a Comanche war party was on the prowl and looking to kill them all. Maybe there was more to them than met the eye. Levi sure could shoot. Rusty figured he would probably beat the old mountain man by next season's Rendezvous. He'd nearly done it this year.

Bill Forrester looked with narrowed eyes at the mountain man who had opened his house to him and his friend. He knew they were all waiting for something similar to what his friend Levi had just done. He knew it would take some doing, and he would need a wagonload of luck for it to all work out, but he had to try. He had the semblance of a plan in mind; all he had to do was put the puzzle together. All defenses were like a puzzle when assembling them. Each piece had its exact place; without every piece where it belonged, you would never see the whole picture. It was his last chance to retain any respect he had as a captain.

"What have we got in the storage basement?" Forrester asked.

The mountain men stared back questioningly. "Why, we got salted pork and potatoes," Angus answered.

"I don't mean food," Forrester replied. "I mean supplies."

"We've got all the things we need to build a house," Rusty said. "You know—hammers, shovels, nails, wire, fuel for the lamps, grease. That and traps. What is it you're lookin' for? The cold cellar is full of stuff we don't want the bears to get to when we ain't here, like this summer when we went down to the Rendezvous."

"Let's go have a look, and I'll tell ya what we can do," Levi said.

Rusty led the way down to the cellar. It was under a trapdoor covered by a rug near the cookstove. Most of the food that needed to keep cool in the summer was stored there. It was the one place bears had never managed to open. He scratched a match across the dinner table and fed the fire to the lamp's wick, which he turned up so they could see in the dark room. Then he disappeared down a ladder, with Forrester right behind.

"Whatcha think he be up to, Beaver?" Angus asked. "If he's as clever as you, I bet it'll be a humdinger of a surprise."

Now, the mountain men seemed more interested in what the two young men had up their sleeves than they did the threat of the Indian attack. Despite their wisdom, they were like children who were being shown magic tricks. Levi had put on a heck of a show. Forrester just hoped that he could come up with something as clever. He had a lot more on the line than his buddy had. He was the one who brought the Sioux to their camp and lost his arm. Now, he had to prove his worth even with his new handicap.

Soon, he was passing hardware from the cellar to the cabin as Levi jumped in to help his best friend. He wanted to see him succeed, even though he knew Bill wasn't skilled in the wilderness like he was. Levi had spent his whole youth living in the forest, isolated with his family in southwestern Indiana.

When they had everything Forrester wanted, they sat before the pile of hardware. Everybody but the young captain had a puzzled look on their faces, including Levi. Nobody had any idea what he was up to, and everybody was curious. Bill had sort of explained what he planned to his best buddy, but he still didn't see how it would work. It seemed too complicated to go at over thirty Sioux Indians.

"I believe first we need to dig some narrow ditches," Levi said. "They need to be all the way around the houses, just two or three feet before the zigzag fence. Give me that can of axle grease and the wooden box, and I'll take care of the rest. Bring that spool of wire with ya, pard, and the bucket of nails. I figure if you boys dig a trench about a foot deep and the width of a spade, it'll suit my needs."

Now, the captain was back. At least, that was what Levi believed. He noticed the change from a broken man to somebody in charge again. He just hoped he had something clever in mind. Half measures wouldn't do this time. Captain Bill Forrester had to pull out all the stops and do something spectacular that would impress their six peers. If they wanted to stay with Rusty, they had to show their worth. Johnson had done just that by running off all the Sioux horses singlehandedly. Bill had something cooked up but had yet to share the whole shebang with his best friend.

"Ain'tcha gonna tell us why we're doin' all this?" Angus asked with a spade in hand. "On second thought, don't tell me. Then it'll come as a surprise." He laughed until he got a stitch. What he thought was so funny was beyond Levi and the captain. They were sweating bullets.

"It's going to be a surprise to the hostile Indians and you boys both," Plain Bill said. "Come on now. We've got to get everything done before the Sioux return. This time it won't be one lone warrior. Levi says there'll be a whole bunch of them."

They were all busy the entire afternoon. All the while, the men kept their eyes on the forest's edge with their rifles within reach. Everyone carried at least two pistols stuffed down their belts. They had locked the horses and mules in the winter stables, so they were harder to steal. Everything that could be taken was stored or tied down. Nobody had any idea of what the Sioux warriors had in mind. They all hoped they hadn't found their horses. Then they would have even more of an advantage.

"Come along, Angus," Rusty Steel said. "These boys are gonna be hungry when they get done diggin' trenches and whatever else Plain Bill wants. Let's make some bacon and biscuits with gravy. I always get a big appetite when I'm waitin' on a little skirmish."

"They must have intended to rush us with the

horses hoping they'd catch us with our britches down around our ankles." Sam snickered. "Iffin it weren't for old Dennis's nose, we'd never have known they were there. I bet you could sniff out truffles before a pig or a dog."

They all laughed. It didn't appear that the threat of hostiles affected the six veteran mountain men much. They had since brought out a jug of whiskey, and they took turns digging ditches and making food. From all appearances, it was just like any other day. They appeared to be repairing the fence. Nobody could imagine what the ditch was for.

When they were done, Bill had them carrying buckets of water to fill the narrow ditch. Finally, Portland Pete brought out some pipe and hooked it up to the water barrels on the side of the house. He siphoned the water off twice as fast as they did with the buckets and saved all the work.

"That does the trick." Rusty laughed. "Whenever confronted with too much work, we can count on Pete here to find an easier way to do things. That trench will be full in no time. I sure hope you don't think you're gonna drown them in twelve inches of water."

They all laughed as they passed around the jug. Levi and Bill never stopped the whole day. At the very end, the captain applied axle grease to the trees along the trails into the compound. The men watching looked more confused with everything he did. He stuck small flour sacks to the grease.

As the day began to come to an end, the light faded, and they didn't quite see everything the young West Point captain was doing. They could only imagine what all those things he was using were for. Nobody had an idea other than Levi, and he wasn't all that sure. They all knew you had to be wicked smart to graduate from such an academy, but they also had run into men who had such educations and were no more than pompous fools. Time would tell if the captain was the real deal or not.

You couldn't get a good run at the buildings from any direction. Much of the vegetation surrounding the cabin was so dense a man would have to hack at it for hours to chop his way through. It was left like that by design rather than chance. It allowed access to a force of more than a couple of warriors only via one of the three regular trails.

Rusty watched carefully as the two young men worked. He had no idea what he was doing out there with Levi, but if he did half as good as Beaver, they should have some entertainment coming their way soon. If any of them were scared, they sure didn't show it. Not like the two young wannabe mountain men. They were as nervous as a cat in a room full of rocking chairs. Both their faces shined with sweat as the sun bore down on the focused young men. Their wet buckskin shirts stuck to their backs.

"I get the feeling that Rusty just invited us up here to stay in his cabin to entertain himself," Bill Forrester said. "He seems to enjoy what we're doing. He never takes his eyes off us. I hope these things I've thought up surprises them like you stealing the horses, Levi. I need to make amends for all the times I've screwed things up."

"What have ya messed up, partner?" Levi asked. "You're too sensitive. I just hope you know what you're doing. I must admit, though, it'll be quite a sight if everything works. You have some imagination, old buddy. If nothing else, it should give a few of the Sioux a heart attack, and a laugh or two will be guaranteed for the old fellas."

Now the two young mountain men laughed. The others sat on the porch smoking cheroots, pipes, and hand-built cigarettes as they wondered what was so funny. The six mountain men were as curious as a raccoon in a garbage bin.

"I sure do hope this works out," Levi said. "Our reputations depend on it."

"You mean my reputation depends on it, don't you?" Forrester said. "I'm just trying not to make a straight line crooked."

"It'd be nice if ya saved us from the Indians, too, while you're at it. We came across Kansas and all the way up here together, Bill," Levi said as he locked eyes with his friend. "I ain't gonna abandon ya no matter how things turn out." Then he smiled. "We've gotta survive the ordeal first before we talk about the future. Now, let's get back at it so we can finish up before dark. If we ain't finished before the Sioux show up, it'll all be for nothin'."

It was nearly dusk when they finished the last bits and pieces. They left four large tin cans beside the fence, near the water trenches. Then Plain Bill began to hang white cloth from fence posts and the porch. He even ran several up cane fishing poles. They looked like little white flags.

When the young friends walked back to the porch, they had all eyes on them. They each stopped, and Bill gave Levi a cheroot—one of two Rusty Steel had given them. They lit them both, making the cinders glow in the deepening darkness. The sun just blushed red on the horizon and disappeared. On the mountains to the east, a full moon peeked over the end of the world. It seemed enormous and so close that you felt you could touch it.

"I believe the Sioux Indians counted on the full moon for the attack tonight," Plain Bill said. "I think they planned to hit us quickly on horseback at either the end of the day or before first light. They would have enough light with the full moon to see where they were going but still be able to create a surprise. It might have worked if we didn't already know they were coming. It was a basic battle plan, really. The element of surprise makes all the difference."

"And why in the world did ya put out all of them white rags?" Angus asked.

"That way, they know that we know they're there," Bill replied. "It's also a universal sign of peace, so maybe we can avoid their attack. When they see we are ready and waiting, plus my surprise, they might turn around and go packing back home."

"You wish," Rusty said. "Them Sioux Indians be a stubborn and ornery bunch. Whatever your surprise is, I sure hope it's big, or there'll be no way to stop thirty-some warriors. I've fought off a few in the past, and they are persistent buggers, they are."

# WAR CHIEF CHASKA

THE REMAINING TWENTY-SIX MEN CAREFULLY NEARED THE three cabins on foot. They knew eight White men occupied them. They also knew they would be heavily armed, having just visited the Rendezvous a month before, where they'd had mountains of furs to trade for the most modern weapons. This was like a knife piercing Chaska's side. All those beavers they trapped came from streams he believed belonged to the Sioux—to his little tribe of Indians.

It certainly didn't belong to the White men. For the North American Indians, the land didn't belong to men. It was men and women who belonged to the land. It had been this way forever. At least until White men came and started marking off property and claiming it for their own, when it belonged to one of the Indian Nations. Even some land that was sacred to different tribes. This mattered little to the progress machine the government had built with its publicity of free land as far away as Ireland, England, and Germany. It was offered right there in the newspapers. They were giving away land they didn't own to people they had never seen. All this was to populate a land full of White people, eliminating the Indians as they came.

Chaska knew that if they had the money from the pelts, they would be the ones with the advanced weapons to turn on them, the very men who sold and made them. He was blinded by the vengeance of his older brother's death, although he claimed it was all for the good of the tribe. In part, it was, so that his intentions weren't totally self-centered.

He knew his people needed more food than they could hunt in the remaining summer months. Once it got cold, hunting was more challenging, and the wolves became dangerous for small groups of hunters or men hunting alone.

Many of his warriors, too, believed it was for the good of the tribe. They couldn't starve while White men lived like kings within traveling distance, with all they needed to eat and piles of cold-weather beaver pelts stacked higher than a man's head. Now, it was time to get back what they felt belonged to them. They were so close they could smell the bacon frying over a fire and the aroma of coffee in the air. The smell of food reminded them of their hungry families back home. It helped to kindle the anger they held inside.

They moved through the night as carefully as they could, with all the stealth they could muster. They were good at hiding but still hadn't learned one of their own tricks. Thirty sweaty men covered in bear grease smelled like the dickens. There was no way they would get close to the cabins before Dennis or Levi smelled them. They should have practiced what they preached.

Chaska took the point, as he was the only one who'd

actually seen the compound. He crawled to the same bush he'd used to spy on them for two full days. When he pushed the leaves aside with his hands, he was surprised to see all eight mountain men on the cabin's porch nearest the trail they were on. They all had rifles across their laps. Two were dozing, but the rest were awake, drinking coffee and smoking pipes. He looked at the yard again confused. *Why was it covered in white flags?* he thought.

Suddenly, he realized they must have known they were there the whole time. Maybe even the two days he watched when he was alone. He apparently thought he was cleverer than he actually was, at least with this bunch. That was when he tied in the loss of the horses to the mountain men. It had to have been one of them and not other Indians. They, too, wore moccasins.

Chaska had been duped into believing this would be a surprise, when all the time they were preparing for their arrival. He didn't miss the fact that if they had ridden holus-bolus toward the cabins on horseback, he might have lost many of his men. At least the first eight shots would have been deadly because they would have come from the sharpshooters' rifles. They all also carried more than one pistol each, and they were probably just as good with them.

Of course, the warriors were expert archers, but he was concerned that no matter how it worked out, he faced the loss of many of his warriors. He wanted to avoid that at all costs, but now he saw no way to do that. The White men had cover that was too good. They had to reach them before they mowed them down. He realized he had lost the most crucial factor of the attack.

That was the element of surprise. His mind began to

spin as he frantically searched for a solution. He had to avoid a massacre. He realized he had just signed his own death warrant. The elders might sing songs of him, but they would not be favorable like he had hoped.

He motioned for his men to spread out and get down while he thought this through, but he kept tight-lipped. It wouldn't do for his men to believe he was without some sort of plan other than running head-on, facing deep dark rifle barrels. As the leader, he didn't doubt he would be among those eight to die first, but he didn't fear for his own life. Now, he feared for the lives of his braves. He also feared for the legacy he wanted to leave. It apparently wasn't going to happen.

They had an hour before first light, so he still had time to think of something to do. He glanced over at the corral, but it was empty. They had even put the horses and mules inside the stables so they would be much harder to steal and safe against arrows. He had to think of a way for this to work. He needed a minor miracle.

His mind raced as he looked in the dark corners of his memory for some experience that would give him a clue as to what he needed to do to come out of this with honor. At that moment, he saw that he was facing a disaster. He would probably be killed, too, especially with the captain inside. He may lop his head off like they said he did to his brother.

He stared at the horizon as his mind continued to race but with no results. Now, he realized what a mistake he had made. Chaska was an honorable man, but he had let restitution obsess and cloud his mind and made some awful decisions. Now, he looked at his men and realized his life was meaningless in the face of losing these friends from his youth. He had lost control of his senses and let revenge take over his very being. He felt humbled before his arrogant mistakes.

The first trace of light was barely visible as the eastern stars began to disappear, and the sky behind them turned light blue. Soon the sun would open its eye on the world, and light would once again dominate this side of the earth. The war chief had run out of time and still had not devised a plan. It was as though his mind had gone blank from the shock of finding the mountain men waiting on him and his braves.

All this he kept to himself and didn't disclose his lack of plans. Things had changed so much all he could see to do was attack head-on. Of course, there was always the option of retreating and returning to camp empty-handed but without loss of life. But of what value would that be to a true warrior like he and his men?

What about the food for the tribe the following winter? There was more at stake here than just his honor and revenge for a death his brother sought. He was between a cliff and a roaring river with a path the width of a hand. His position was precarious, to say the least.

He looked across his men's solemn faces as he saw what would be. They, too, had a warrior's fire in their eyes. The braves were biting at the bit to run for their enemies. You could see it in their faces. They longed to kill everyone they could before giving their lives like brave warriors were expected to do.

*May the spirits protect us,* Chaska thought. He dug in his feet and raced toward the wooden fence and the cabins behind. His legs were a blur as he ran in a burst of speed for his life. His Sioux warriors followed as they screamed their war cries. The silence suddenly disappeared and was now full of frightening screams of battle. Now there was no need for stealth.

Maybe their war cries would send a bolt of terror through the mountain men's souls. Chaska knew he was on the side of right and not that of wrong. He ran toward his own demise like his hair was on fire.

Just as he closed in on the wood post fence, he saw the silhouettes of two men. He only noticed them because of the cigars they held in their hands. The smell of harsh tobacco was strong in the air. They flicked the fiery embers into a small ditch right after they kicked several large tin cans over. Nothing made any sense, so Chaska continued to run.

He didn't know what else to do. He was a warrior, after all, so he did what he knew best. He was ready to fight, so he focused on the task at hand and launched forward like a raging bull.

# SURPRISES

ONCE BILL AND LEVI HAD EVERYTHING READY, THEY returned to the porch. The large round table was covered in steaming hot biscuits and a massive bowl of gravy. They had been sliced open, and slabs of fried bacon slapped in the middle. A gallon pot of hot coffee sat on the table as steam spewed from the spout, spreading the aroma through the air. Each man grabbed a tin pie pan from the stack. Everyone had their own knife, fork, and spoon, which they always carried. A mountain man never knew when or where he would eat next, and it was more hygienic, although hygiene wasn't usually at the top of their list of necessities.

"So, have you two got everything ready for that bunch of rascals iffin they show up tonight?" Rusty Steel asked. "We'll be ready all right, but that's a mighty big war party you're talkin' about. Maybe we should all get inside and batten down the hatches."

"Hatches?" Levi asked.

"That's seaman's talk for doors and windows." Rusty smiled. "Remember, I was a captain once, too, and that didn't work out for me either, but unlike you, Plain Bill, I lost my boat and all my men to French pirates. They were actually more like simple thieves and scallywags."

"I believe it will be tonight or tomorrow morning," Forrester said. "There will be a full moon, so they will have fair visibility. My best guess would be in the morning, just before the first stars disappear. Morning battles are preferable, so if things aren't finished fast, they can see to plan their next move. It also gives them time to arrive quietly and set up before they attack. At least, that's what I would do. Then again, I would never attack men like us with modern weapons even if there are thirty-some Indians."

"I reckon we'll all be spending the night here on the porch then," Rusty said as he scraped a wooden match on the table. It crackled to life with a blue-yellow flame. The smell of sulfur filled the air. He lit the lamp with the wick down low to limit the glow to a dull yellow light that circled the porch. Each man had a rifle in his lap or handy nearby.

For ten minutes, nobody said a word as they shoveled food into their mouths. Finally, forks scraped empty pie pans, and in the blink of an eye, there wasn't a scrap of food left on the table. They all sat back, and Angus poured coffee all around; then came a jug of corn liquor to spike their evening java.

Levi passed the jug without pouring himself a smidgen.

"What's the matter, Beaver?" Angus asked. "Are ya sayin' you don't drink with the likes of us?"

"I just wanna stay as sharp as I can in case the Sioux attack us at night," Levi replied as his eyes traced the tree line at the edge of their clearing. "That fella guardin' the Indian's horses was drinkin' too and look what it got him. He fell asleep on the job and lost all their animals."

"Don't worry so much, young fella," Angus said. "A little dash will do ya a world of good. It'll take that nervous energy ya got eatin' at your stomach down a notch or two. You don't see any of us worried, do ya?"

"So, why don't you worry, Angus?" Levi asked. "I thought everybody worried some."

"Yeah, but most folks have expectations." Angus smiled. "Iffin you're not expectin' nothin', there ain't nothin' to worry about."

"From my past experiences, the hostile Indians are fierce, so naturally, I worry about 'em all," Levi said.

"Yeah, I figured as much," Angus replied. "And how's that workin' out for ya, pilgrim? Did all that worrying change anything up till now—anything at all?"

"So what about preparing for the future?" Levi asked. The train of thought of these rugged men who chose to live in the wilderness puzzled him.

"How much more prepared do ya want us to get? We've loaded our guns, and Plain Bill has done his bit, so what more is there to do?" Angus asked. Now he was the one looking confused.

"Ain't you worried about the hostiles?" Levi asked. He was so worried about what was to come, his stomach was doing flip-flops.

"Why should I be?" Angus asked. "They ain't here yet, are they? We don't even know for sure that they're even comin' at all."

The perplexed expression on Levi's face deepened. He couldn't grasp the way the mountain men thought. Not thinking about the past or worrying about the future seemed to be against human nature, but they all did seem content, and not a single one showed any sign of nervousness. They were as calm as a millpond. There wasn't even the slightest ripple. Again, he had to ask himself what kind of men they were. He certainly hadn't met their equals on his journey west.

Crickets chattered in the dark as coyotes sang their choir. The massive moon cast a silver glow over the mountains. Three raccoons ducked under the fence and raced across the clearing, oblivious to the men sitting there with guns. Their eyes followed them as they disappeared under the fence on the opposite side. Nobody paid them any mind.

"I smell a skunk," Dennis said.

"Whatcha mean ya smell a skunk?" Rusty asked. "What did I do wrong now?"

"It's simple enough, fool. I smell a polecat. Can't you boys smell nothing?"

Bill just shrugged, but Levi closed his eyes and imagined a skunk in his mind. He identified all the other odors one by one and then blocked them all out. That was when Levi smelled the faintest scent of a skunk. He wondered if he had an exceptional talent like Dennis with his ability to sniff things out. Maybe he was better skilled for the wilderness than he had thought.

His sense of smell instantly changed; he smelled everything, where it came from and what it was. It was like a blind man suddenly receiving the miracle of sight. It opened his mind to one of his senses that he considered less critical for survival than it was. It was almost like he had gained another sense; such was the detail in his mind when he closed his eyes and breathed. Dennis was who'd warned them of the Sioux in the first place.

Now he saw how important his sense of smell was in the wilderness. He could probably smell bears before they came into sight. He became more of a mountain man with each passing day.

"I smell it," Levi whispered, amazed at his discovery. "It was always there, but I never tried, so I didn't know I could smell things so well. I can even separate them and tell where the smell comes from."

"Well, I'll be if this young fella ain't gonna outdo us all before long." Rusty chuckled. "Remember, it was me who brought him along. I must say that I always have been a good judge of character."

"Even a blind pig can find a truffle once in a while," Mountain Dennis said and laughed.

That long night they sat around the table telling tales and probably a good dose of lies to the two young wannabe mountain men. They both gobbled up information like hungry wolves. Every once in a while, Plain Bill would fill the small ditch that surrounded the compound as the earth absorbed the water, but it had rained a lot that summer and the ground was wet already, so the water stood for hours before seeping into the soggy mud.

They had no idea what the rest of Forrester's surprise was. They tried to guess what the water was for, but the young captain kept tight-lipped and refused to give his secrets away. He said it would take the surprise out of the maneuver. Rusty Steel was happy to wait. For him, this was just a bit more entertainment. After the Rendezvous, something was always happening with the two newcomers.

For the briefest moment, Rusty wondered why he had brought them. Then he smiled and knew it was for the fun of watching them learn or fail—maybe that and curiosity about this new young mountain man, Levi Beaver Johnson. He was the first man he had met that shot a rifle better than him. He was nearly as skilled as the six men who lived in the compound, and it had taken them over a decade to learn what this huge young fellow learned in a few months.

All night long, the stories flowed as one mountain man tried to outdo another. By the end, both Levi and Bill believed it was all lies. They described things that couldn't possibly have happened even up here in the mountains. Then again, many things had happened since they hit Kansas that they never would have imagined. Life in the mountains was so shrouded with mystery a man had to learn from his daily experiences and not much more, but Levi had a natural knack for all things a path maker and frontiersman should know.

Angus and Pete sat dozing on their chairs; the former snored lightly. They had dragged them over to the wall and pushed them back as their feet dangled. They rested their heads on the siding and dozed off and on. They still had their Hawken rifles in their fists, so that if even a twig broke, they would be ready instantly.

Levi and Dennis sat on the edge of the porch staring out into the dark. The trees moved with the breeze, making dark shadows dance on the buildings. Dennis took a whiff of air, but he smelled nothing out of place. He shrugged and walked to the side of the cabin to take a leak.

Beaver Johnson closed his eyes like he'd done before and took a deep breath. He identified each odor, then separated two and frowned.

"We've got company," Levi whispered.

Dennis buttoned up his britches and grabbed the gun he had leaned against the wall. Then he smelled it too.

"I smell sweaty men and somethin' that stinks even worse than that," Levi whispered. "It kind of smells like grease."

"That'll be the bear fat the Indians rub into their skin," Dennis said and stifled a chuckle. "It's supposed to keep them warm on cool nights and in the winter. It's common enough among the mountain tribes where it gets cold like here." He shot a glance over his shoulder and said, "Wake up, you two. We've got company, and I doubt they're friendly types."

Levi and Bill immediately puffed the cigars to life they had lit earlier. Smoke billowed around their heads. Nobody had ever seen such giant cheroots. The cinders were the size of a fat man's thumb. They moved through the shadows toward the fence in front of the house. Then they kicked the kerosene cans over, spilling them into the water. They tossed the hot embers in, and flames raced around the compound as if by magic. The flammable fluid was lighter, so the four kerosene tins covered the water in the ditch all the way around the cabins. It looked like a magic trick from a circus. By design, it was intended to distract the warriors.

Suddenly, they could see the Sioux Indians running toward them with their bows in hand. They were stringing arrows as they neared the burning trench. The confidence on their faces diminished. After two days, the war paint had run in streaks; now, they all appeared dirty rather than ferocious. As the fire raced around the compound, it put the fear of the wraith in their souls.

The Indians thought it was black magic, just like Forrester had hoped.

When they'd almost reached the burning pits, they tripped over the wire Bill and Levi had strung from tree to tree just at the edge of the clearing. Then they'd covered the tripwire with dry leaves. That way, combined with the shock of the fire, the attacking warriors didn't look down. The first dozen fell on their faces in their rush for the cabin. The rest piled up behind them.

So far, not one of the mountain men had moved a muscle, and all of them had grins on their faces. They weren't afraid of Indians or much of anything else. They must be so bored up there in the mountains that they used whatever they had for personal entertainment.

Levi raised his rifle and took a bead. He pulled the trigger. The gun bucked hard. Flame and smoke chased the chunk of lead out of the barrel and across the clearing to the tree. When the bullet hit the dynamite held to the trunk by axle grease, it exploded, breaking the tree in two. From ten feet and up, it fell across the trail and on top of the approaching enemy. A spray of nails flew through the air. If they had come by horse, the men at the front would have been dead along with the horses.

Forrester passed a second loaded gun to Levi, and he took another shot. Another tree exploded as the stick of dynamite went off. It deafened the Sioux warriors and left them confused and disoriented. When the second tree fell, it trapped the Sioux on this side of the forest. The trail was covered and unpassable. Some were pinned down between the fallen limbs. The mountain men with rifles just sat there and grinned. It was like they were at the theater watching a play, waiting to see what happened in the end.

Things didn't go as Chaska had planned. With the mountain men knowing they were coming and waiting armed, the element of surprise was eliminated, and it completely ruined his plans. All it took was one wrong turn on the trail, and everything fell to pieces.

It was evident through the haze that the war chief wasn't sure what had happened or what he had done. Black smoke poured from the tiny mote around the compound as the kerosene burned itself out. Some warriors staggered around in circles while others sat on their backsides with confused expressions on their faces. They were covered in dirt and dust from head to toe and in every wrinkle. It stuck to their war paint. A single tear of frustration ran down Chaska's face, cutting a path through the mud.

The White men watched him try to shake the cobwebs away and blink his eyes. One brave stood, took two steps, and dropped to his knees, finally sitting on his feet. He was too dazed from the blast and couldn't stay upright. It was all he could do to remain conscious, and he was totally deaf from the explosion. Blood ran out of one of his ears.

Plain Bill Forrester had put the dynamite too high to kill the Indians unless they came at them on horseback. That would have taken the risk up a notch. He intended to scare them more than anything if he could and force them into retreating. The whole idea of the fire was to make them think it was black magic and evil spirits at work. The hidden wire they had strung was covered with dry leaves. He knew the first men would fall on their faces before the dynamite went off, saving their lives, although the explosion was more potent than Bill had expected. His ears rang loudly in his head. Luckily nobody was killed, and his plan worked like clockwork. He felt he had redeemed himself in front of his new peers. Now, he began to feel like an equal and ignored his empty sleeve. It wasn't going to grow back, so he had better get used to it.

# Hunters &
# Gatherers

When the mountain men saw how dazed and confused the Sioux warriors were, they jumped to action and captured the bunch. To the captain's surprise, it was easy as moving a herd of milk cows. All two dozen Indians were so shell-shocked they walked around like zombies, bouncing into each other, confused. Some had a loss of hearing and other vertigo and could hardly stand up without falling over again. Others had cuts, bruises, and scratches from flying splinters—a few others from nails. Some still had some fire in their eyes, but it wasn't the chief. Sure, he was confused too. Who wouldn't be with such a display as Forrester organized?

At least no one was dead, and that was the primary plan. Bill had thought if they could capture the Indians without a shot fired, there was a chance of negotiation. He knew some of them came after him for the death of the Sioux warrior. That he could see clearly, but he doubted there were more than one or two family members in the war party.

The others must have another reason to travel so far to kill a single White man. It couldn't all be about revenge. Captain Forrester felt he had lost enough men and killed enough Indians to last him a lifetime. If he could turn this around and not shed blood, all the better. He had enough weight on his shoulders from the men he'd lost and the Indians he'd had to kill. When they hit western Kansas, everywhere they went things seemed violent and dangerous beyond their wildest dreams.

In minutes, they had them rounded up with their hands tied. They looped each one to another so if one ran, they would all fall. Nobody made a violent action toward anyone. Not the mountain men toward the Indians nor the Sioux toward the White men. The only sign of aggression was the initial attack. The braves were too stunned and shaken from the two blasts and the instant failure of their planned attack to react. Some still questioned where they were. Others stumbled around without realizing what had happened or what they were doing there. Their attack didn't even reach the compound's fence, let alone riding a horse into the cabin as Chaska had dreamed.

Levi recognized the warrior who had been spying on them. He remembered the leaves braided into his hair. They were still there. He instantly saw he was the leader when all his warriors turned their eyes toward him with questioning faces.

"Do any of you men speak English?" Bill Forrester called out.

He didn't hesitate and naturally took command of the situation and the possible prisoners. Time would tell if they were to be friends or foes.

"I speak English. I am Sioux War Chief Chaska. It means *First Born*."

"Where did you learn to speak such good English?" Levi asked. He wasn't shy at all. His curiosity already had the best of him.

"When I was young, my father taught me to know my enemies. How can you really know an enemy if you don't understand what he says? Only then do you understand his thoughts and strengths and weaknesses. Only then are you prepared to fight."

"It looks like you did a pretty poor job of figuring out how Levi and Plain Bill here think," Dennis said. "You may understand most White folks by their words, but you won't find many mountain men that you'll understand by how they speak. We judge men by what they do and not what they say."

"I believe you came here to kill me, didn't you, Chief Chaska?" Captain Forrester asked. "What do you want to do about that? I'm open to suggestions. I had no intention of killing your brother. I didn't invite him or challenge him. He came here and challenged me and left me with no choice in the matter. If the truth is known, I didn't believe I would win the battle, either. I believe I got lucky." He looked down at his empty sleeve. "Or at least luckier than your brother. I was a captain in the Army, and we were supposed to fight Indians, but I lost my taste for the job right away. Now, I just want to live in peace here on this mountain. Or is there something else that brought all your fighters all this way?"

"We were jealous because your streams are full of beaver, and ours are all trapped out. There are still elk here, and near our camp, there are none," Chaska said. "With White men living on Indian land, it seemed wrong when our people starve, and you have full bellies."

Rusty nodded and stood and said, "Why, any man would fight iffin they didn't have food to feed their families. If it's grub or pelts y'all need, why didn't ya try askin'? We would have probably obliged. It is true—we have more than we need this year."

Rusty hadn't taken his eyes off the Indians the whole time. He had been sitting and watching everything that had happened. The explosion surprised him, too, but you wouldn't have noticed because he didn't even flinch or twitch. Nothing seemed to surprise Rusty other than man's stupidity. That was something he often pointed out.

Of the six mountain men, he was the one with the most wisdom in his eyes. Most of the time, it wasn't noticeable, but you could see how sincere he was when he was serious. He had been an orphan and lived on the streets of St. Louis, begging for scraps of food and whatever he could steal. He was a thief until a gentleman forgave him for a crime and gave him a second chance. He provided him with a job, two square meals a day, and a roof over his head.

He also collected a few pennies at the end of the month for something special or to save. He also gave him a profession, and eventually, he bought his own boat. He knew how it was to be hungry for days, and nobody helped or cared. Maybe he could do something about this poor tribe. It had been a long time since he'd helped the hungry. It looked like the time had come again.

"If you're hungry, we can all go out and hunt for your folks for the comin' winter. We've got the best two shots in the mountains." Angus laughed. "If y'all will set your anger aside for a moment, we may be able to save your people a bad winter."

Chaska blinked his eyes repeatedly. He seemed more confused and puzzled than ever. He had been defeated without a single shot fired, and he still couldn't figure out how it happened. As he stood there listening to the generosity offered by the men he intended to murder, the anger for his brother's death seemed to lessen. He knew his brother well enough to know he was a glory seeker. Apparently, fame was more important to him than his life because he gave it up for nothing. The elders sang no songs of his brother or his death. Men who lose aren't remembered. Only dead winners make it to the elder's songs. History is always written by the victors.

All the anger drained away from Chaska like someone had pulled the plug on a tub, and it swirled down and out the drain. He suddenly felt a heavy weight lift from his shoulders. His foggy mind cleared, and he realized the older man with the fuzzy beard was speaking to him. The White men had quickly figured out he was the leader. What else didn't they know about them already? It was still a mystery how they had found out they were watching. Nobody had ever caught Chaska hiding in a blind. Maybe he wasn't as good as he thought, or maybe these men were better than any others he had known.

"Whatcha say, Chaska?" Rusty asked. "Your folks look mighty puzzled. Why don't cha tell 'em what's goin' on and see iffin they think it's fair."

"You probably run out of beaver by overhunting. The same goes with all game animals," Dennis said. "I seen it happen to a Crow camp a few years back. You have to watch how many animals you take, or they won't be able to reproduce, and you ruin your forests. I ain't sayin' ya have. Of course, here we were, only six, and are still only eight. That's nothing compared to even a small tribe. But just the same, I can understand where you're comin' from. It ain't so much as you're overhunting, but you've made your camp in a place without a plentiful food supply. If you overhunt, it ain't sustainable. That's the first thing I looked for when I settled here over ten years ago. Why have y'all taken so long to come and visit?"

"I came for both reasons," Chaska nearly whispered. "I had my plans clear, but you were all three steps ahead of me. I still don't quite understand what happened."

"Go ahead and talk to your men," Levi said. "Let's see what they think about the offer. Y'all ain't in the best position in the world to dictate, but just the same, we'll listen. Whatcha say, Bill?"

He was startled, like he was deep in thought about something. He did a double take, thought about the question, and said, "Yeah, of course. Anything is better than more killing. I just don't have it in me today."

"Why, you saved the day," Rusty laughed. His laugh was deep and resonated as it bounced off the canyon walls. "That surprise you set up was the dangest thing I've ever seen. From now on, we'll call you Plainsman Bill instead of just Plain Bill." He laughed again and pulled on his beard.

"Go and see what your warriors say about our offer," Levi said to Chaska. "I hope you don't have any trouble convincing 'em. I know we tied y'all up and all, but ya did attack our camp. Most White folks would have just as soon shot ya."

Angus sat on the porch but still had his rifle in hand, just like Syracuse Sam, who sat beside him.

"I've already been scalped once, and I don't aim to let it happen again," he whispered as he drew back the hammer on his Hawken rifle.

"Hold your horses, pard," Angus replied. "Let's see what Rusty and that new boy work out. Both of those young men seem to be clever rascals in different ways. But I ain't too sure them Sioux will agree to what we're offerin'. They're askin' for the whole hog, and we're offerin' 'em pork chops."

Finally, Chaska spoke. He cleared his throat, and his first words came out with less confidence than he would have liked. He said, "I'll tell my people what is happening. I will also tell them what you said. Your suggestion might solve our problem for a short time, but next year we may have the same issues again. Then what will we do? Come back and ask for more? Our people are too proud to be beggars."

"Sometimes begging is better than bein' a thief," Rusty said. "I should know because, as a boy, I was an orphan on the St. Louis docks. When I begged, I ate less than when I stole, but I did get beat up for taking what wasn't mine."

Chaska nodded and slowly turned and walked over to where his men sat. They had plenty of rope to move around but not enough to charge the mountain men if they decided to have a go. Most of them were puzzled and didn't understand how they'd fallen into the hands of the White men so fast. They were also curious about what Chaska was saying. They all knew he had learned the White man's English. They had thought it foolish at the time. They'd never thought there would be White men like army ants as they ate their way across the plains.

"Whatcha think those warriors are gonna think about our offer?" Angus asked. He looked from Dennis to Rusty.

"How would I know?" Rusty spat. "I ain't no gypsy fortune teller. We're gonna have to wait, but keep your guns handy, boys. Some of the Sioux don't look like they lost all their fight yet. Some of them still have scrappy eyes."

# FIGHT OR FLIGHT

CHASKA FINISHED TALKING TO THE WHITE MEN, AND HE was dreading what was to come next. He turned around and faced his men. He moved one foot in front of the other. They weighed like a ton of lead. Now he had to find some way to tell his people how miserably they had lost without angering some of the testier warriors. It had been an utter disaster, but strangely, nobody was killed or even seriously injured. He still didn't understand the details of how they did it, but in a couple of seconds, they went from a fierce charging Sioux war party to what resembled a confused herd of buffalo.

Black Mink stood at the head of the warriors, and he didn't even try to hide his anger. Of course, he blamed Chaska for losing the battle so badly and so quickly. It was over before they shot their first arrow. Nobody even fired a gun. He was disappointed in everything. He had expected to do battle and win in all the glory. Instead, they were tied up with eight men with guns as big as cannons standing watch on them. They felt they would die if they tried to escape.

"I don't have much to say," Chaska said. He still held his chin high and maintained his pride, although his words sounded hollow. "We lost because our enemy was cleverer than us—or me. We would generally suffer consequences, but these men don't seem interested in killing us. They said they wanted to help us hunt and gather supplies for the coming winter."

"Sure, and what about next year?" Black Mink spat.

"It's a trick, for sure," Spotted Dog said. "I don't trust any White men. It has to be more magic, like the fire surrounding the compound. How could something like that happen? But watch what they promise because nothing they promise is ever true. Promises—promises for everything, just like now. What have they promised you, Chaska?" He said it like it was an accusation.

Usually, the war chief would have struck him then and there, but now he had to be diplomatic. He knew he could bring the majority to his side, but some of his best warriors would refuse to agree. They came all this way to fight, not make deals with liars and thieves. Chaska had to admit everything the White chiefs had promised had turned out to be lies, so why should they believe these eight mountain men? Sure, they lived like Indians except for their lodges. They liked to make them prominent and permanent when it was best to have a house you could move from one place to another like the Sioux. The wilderness was full of surprises, and they all knew any number of things could make a tribe move—especially food.

"I don't know what kind of magic they made to capture us so easily, but if we want to live, we better respect them, or we may end up dead," Chaska said.

"They offered peace and help to feed our people. What are we going to offer them in return?"

"If they don't want to kill us and offered to help us with food, I don't see why we should fight," White Weasel said. "Especially now that we know how dangerous these men are."

"If they bleed red, we can kill them," Black Mink spat. "I'm not afraid of any White men—mountain men or not. That wasn't magic when we arrived. Those were tricks. These men don't look like medicine men or shamans. They are no more than White trappers, and they are stealing our beaver pelts."

"I'm all ears if you have an idea of how to get out of this alive and still have the land to trap and hunt," Chaska said in a calm, even voice. "Is that what you want, Black Mink?"

"It wouldn't be hard to do better than you," Black Mink growled. He didn't hide his disdain for the war chief. He knew he wouldn't make the mistakes he did. All he needed was a chance.

"We can take a vote—I am willing to lead those that want to follow me," Chaska said. "Those that don't, I won't look at them with anger, but will understand."

"Let's see who our men want to follow. You, Chaska, a loser, or me? I have yet to be a war chief, but I can promise I can do better than we have done so far."

Chaska stood silently by. He knew he had said all he could. The Sioux weren't like Americans, who would discuss things for days. Indians often make snap decisions, especially in a losing battle that could cost lives. The problem was he knew he was passing the situation on to a man of lesser wisdom. He just hoped destiny was on his side this day, or he might not live to see the sunset.

Chaska walked over to a tree stump and sat down. He turned his back on his people. He could hear Black Mink brag and tell them how he would figure out how to defeat the White men who held them. Strangely enough, they still didn't understand they had already been defeated, and the offer for food and a promise not to take any lives was a clemency they should not shun. But as always, the majority ruled in their tribe. Back in the stronghold, it was voted on among the elders. On the battlefield, it was decided right then and there between warriors.

Often a leader is killed, and they had to decide who leads in his footsteps after he falls. This was a different situation but still within the norms of their society. Of course, if they tried to do such a thing to a chief, it would mean their scalps, but a failed war chief could fall victim to an aggrieved war party.

He tried to block out the criticism Black Mink was dishing out. He accused Chaska of everything. *Maybe it was true*, he thought to himself. He had been sure he wasn't seen, when obviously he was. Perhaps he was losing his touch and should step down peacefully. Of course, if he wanted to challenge Black Mink, he could, but it would mean a battle to the death of one or the other. He didn't wish any harm to a man he had known most of his life. The greed for power and position had bitten Black Mink, affecting his judgment.

*Judgment?* Chaska thought. *Good judgment was precisely what he was apparently lacking.* He made no speeches nor tried to convince any of his men to follow him. He felt they would never know him if they didn't know him by now. So let be it judged by destiny, and they would accept whatever was to be.

Black Mink stood on a tree stump and encouraged the men to join him. This proved to be a hard sell with the warriors all tied together. At least he had a captive audience. In the end, he only got four men to follow him on whatever plan he thought up. The rest stayed loyal to Chaska. He heard footsteps behind him, and he knew. Before they voted, he knew who would betray him and who wouldn't. Now he would have to look out for Black Mink and his pack of wolves. He didn't want to mess things up and have the White men turn on them. He knew they could never win.

After seeing how sturdy their buildings were and apparently well stocked, he now saw that even if the horses hadn't been run off, he still would have failed a frontal rush. Their homes were like small forts, and with closed doors and shutters, they were nearly impenetrable. He also recognized the rifles. A couple of Sioux chiefs used the same gun. It was so powerful it could kill a buffalo with a single shot. Not to mention how they'd used the dynamite to trap them in seconds. These were opponents who were as dangerous as they come.

It was also apparent that one of them was very clever and knew how to stop them dead in their tracks as soon as they attacked. They would never defeat such a brilliant man. He still didn't know exactly what had happened other than the dynamite. He wondered how he got it to stick to the trees.

When Chaska turned around, five warriors turned their back on him. The rest looked questioningly. Of course, they wondered what would come next. The other five showed their defiance despite being bound and tied together. He hoped they didn't ruin things for them all. It would be a shame if he managed to make a truce only to have Black Mink ruin it by doing something stupid. Each warrior brave could do what they wanted, though. They often even did things the tribe's principal chiefs tell them not to. They were fierce and somewhat unpredictable.

He would have to watch carefully so he could hamper their attempt if they did get a chance.

"I believe these White people are honest and really want to help us," Chaska said. "I trust them. At least until they prove otherwise. They said they would hunt with us so we have food for the long winter months. They have good rifles and say they are expert shots. They can kill elk from much farther than our bow and arrows. We will work with them and give peace a chance. If it proves they are false, like most White men we have met, we can fight even if they have to die. We can never accept to be prisoners."

The loosely tied ropes with lots of slack allowed the five Sioux warriors that decided to go against Chaska to gravitate toward each other. Finally, they were in a huddle, undoubtedly making a plan. Chaska knew Black Mink was brave and not at all dumb. He hoped he showed common sense when dealing with the White men. He doubted that they suffered fools.

Chaska shot a glance over his shoulder and saw the White men waiting on the porch for an answer. He would speak to them with the majority rule. Their vote allowed him to speak for his people. They were all aware that Black Mink would drop them in the mud if he made the wrong move when they attempted their escape. He doubted they would try to defeat the eight mountain men. They would eat the five Sioux warriors for lunch and ask for seconds.

He turned toward the White men and smiled, but the smile didn't reach his eyes. He was troubled because his next moves would determine the future of him and his men. He knew he couldn't throw Black Mink under a wagon and tell the White men he planned against them. He was part of the tribe, and that would be unforgivable. All he could do was wish and hope that he didn't do anything too stupid and get any of those who chose peace over war to suffer for his actions.

Those that voted to join him would also have their destinies. Theirs would be different. He hoped and prayed to the spirits nothing would happen to turn the White men on the innocent. If he did, they would all die in the blink of an eye.

# THE HUNT

Now that everybody agreed, they attempted to organize a hunt. Rusty and Dennis eyed the Sioux with suspicion. There were more of them than the mountain men. Now they had to rely on the word of Chaska, a war chief they had never even heard of.

"We're gonna have to cut the Sioux free, or they ain't gonna be huntin' much," Levi said. "I reckon of the lot, there be a couple or three that don't like how things panned out, but if we keep an eye out, we should be able to spot trouble before it blossoms. These Indians don't seem to be nearly as hard as the Comanche were."

"Comanche?" Rusty said. "Why is everybody afraid of Comanche. That ain't no secret. Those very fellas in front of us wouldn't be so brave iffin we were Comanche. Just look at how they look at me whenever I say the word. We're all lucky we're alive."

Chaska heard the last part of the conversation as he neared the porch. "Did you say there are Comanche around here?"

"What'd I tell ya." Rusty snickered. "No, we left the

Comanche back in west Kansas. There ain't nothin' but Crow. Blackfeet and Ute up here. I rarely see a Sioux, either. You folks must have a tiny village if we ain't run into it."

"We only number a hundred or so," Chaska said. "The men here are all of our warriors and hunters. Some, like me, do both because we don't have enough to eat. What do you plan to do now?"

Rusty looked Chaska up and down like he was evaluating him as a man and his honor. "I reckon we ain't got many choices. It's either trust ya, and we all go huntin', or we have to kill ya all to make sure you don't come back on us with bad intentions."

"I give you my word as a warrior that my people and I won't try to run away or rebel," Chaska said. "Just note that all my warriors didn't agree with what I proposed, but most of them did. Of twenty-six, only five said no."

Dennis eyed the Indians all tied together and looked each one up and down. He finally said, "That tall warrior with that big frown must be one."

"That is Black Mink," Chaska said. "He is the leader of those against my decision. I can't guarantee what he will do. If he does nothing, the men with him will not act alone. They won't have the courage or are not as foolish as Black Mink."

"Maybe we should tie 'em up and leave 'em in the cold cellar," Dennis said. "If we put a barrel over it, he won't get out until we return, anyway."

"It's a dodgy business dealing with angry warriors," Angus said. "I had a run-in with a few strappy Crow who didn't want me in the camp when I married my Crow wife. I talked to Green Leaves, and she talked to the chief, and he said he couldn't act until one of the warriors got violent. Most of 'em brag about who they can kill and how they are better than the others. It's a competitive business when you're a war party."

"Well, how are we gonna go about this then?" Levi asked. "If we know who's a troublemaker, it will be an insult if we do anything to him before he strikes out at us. Heck, then it could be too late."

Captain Forrester stood silent the whole time as he listened to the others and thought about the problem. "When we were still riding for the Army, Levi would go out and shoot game and several men followed with mules and gutted and skinned the animals, so they were ready to return to camp. If Black Mink is put on the gutting and skinnin' detail, then he won't need a bow and arrow. He can get by with a knife. Do you men think we can control one warrior without his bow and arrow? I doubt he be a daisy, but I don't see one man going up against us all with a knife in his hand. He would have to be so brave he'd be crazy."

"That's clever thinking, Bill," Rusty said.

He had stopped calling him Plain Bill because he, like Levi, had shown his worth and then some. Both men had been silently accepted into the family of the mountain men. Nobody made an announcement or made any mention of it at all. But the two new members of the group could tell. The hacking stopped, and they spoke to them like their opinions mattered.

"Whatcha think, Beaver?" Angus asked. "Do you think these boys can be watched and trusted with a knife? Who are the other four that said they wanted to follow that fool?" They all looked at Chaska again.

"I can't bring myself to be a...what is the word I'm looking for? I think you call them rats. Men who tell on others to gain position or to trick others into doing what they don't want to do."

"That's hogwash," Portland Pete retorted. "Iffin they pose a threat to any one of us, we should act first and ask questions later."

"Do you really want to wipe out a small tribe of Sioux?" Rusty Steel asked. "You know there be other camps of Sioux, especially toward Montana. If we get them riled up enough, they may decide to take the loss of a poor camp as aggression, and a hundred warriors could come down on us. If we do the right thing here, we may just make peace with the same people who wanted to run us off. Once they see we ain't out to make their people suffer and are willin' to help, I believe even the ones that voted against Chaska will see the light. I know Levi can scare up enough game to make 'em happy for now. Maybe we can leave some more grub by their camp before the summer's over."

"I see you understand part of my problem," Chaska said. "It is hard for a war chief to keep all his warriors together after a failed attempt."

"That failed attempt kept your lot from gettin' killed," Levi said. "Iffin you would have rushed us like you planned, not even your horses would have survived. By the by, did you find your animals? Anybody in your war party that don't see that is either blind or a danged fool."

"The eight of us can hunt with rifles, and we'll keep our pistols ready in case Black Mink makes a break for it or tries to attack one of us," Forrester said. "He won't get far with a skinning knife. We best be the ones who pick out who does what, so the chief here doesn't get blamed. Nobody needs to know you gave your man up, and don't beat yourself up about it. You have probably saved some of your warriors by telling us where the danger is. If we didn't know, it would be easy for things to get out of control, and y'all get killed. It only takes a few seconds for everything to fall apart. We all know how hard that was for you to do. But it was the only way you were gonna save your people from getting hurt."

"My reputation is so damaged now it matters little to me at this point," Chaska said. "I have made too many mistakes with my plans to run you men off. Now I realize you meant no harm." He locked eyes with Forrester and said, "I know you had no choice with my older brother. He had always been a little like Black Mink. That was why he never made it to be a war chief. You don't only have to show bravery and cunning, you also have to show how you protect your men in dangerous situations. I just hope that I'm making the right decision now."

"You've made the only decision you could and didn't foolishly sacrifice your people for an impossible task," Levi said. "I haven't been a mountain man so long like the other men here, but I can assure you they are as brave and scrappy as any men I've ever seen. You might have killed one or two of us, but you would have never succeeded. If for nothing more than because of our superior firepower and our impenetrable cover in the cabins. It would be like attacking a small fort."

"I was counting on the element of surprise," Chaska said.

"Next time you want to surprise some clever White men, try washing off all that bear fat." Dennis chuckled like it was all just a joke. The mountain men still seemed only to take the situation half seriously. "I

smelled ya the first day you were out there spyin' on us.
That was what gave ya up. It's just like you folks sniff us
out because some stupid fools use smelly soap to wash.
The same thing works if you are up against knowledge-
able men. Even Levi smelled ya in the end. We knew
you were coming well before you were in sight. The two
of us got powerful strong senses of smell."

"You're gonna have to get up earlier in the morning
iffin ya want to sneak up on us and catch us out, Chaska." Angus laughed at the situation. He had never seen
an Indian ambush that worked out so poorly for the
assailants. Lucky for them, they were well ready, and
Bill saved the day, so nobody got shot. Not even the
Sioux. At least yet.

# TRUST & HONOR

THEY SEPARATED THE WARRIORS INTO THREE GROUPS. They let Chaska select who would go with whom, hoping he kept the five dubious braves that voted no from the others. As they were going hunting, they were all well-armed, and the Sioux warriors had only skinning and carving knives to gut, skin, and cut the meat from each animal they bagged. They led mules as they walked behind the mountain men.

"What happened to those horses y'all had that I spooked and ran off?" Levi asked. He couldn't help but make a little smile. "You must have been able to catch a few. They couldn't have gone that far away."

"They ran farther than you would think," Chaska said. "They were too close to the Crow camp to take the risk. We knew we couldn't fight the Crow Indians and you mountain men at the same time. Our horses were all nags and old anyway. It wasn't that much of a loss. We lost more pride than we did possessions. That stings even to the humblest warrior or hunter. If we can return to our camp with food, most of the tribe will forget we also went for revenge. Hunger will do that to you.

"When a man is starving, he only thinks about acquiring food. Hunger will do that to you. If we can fill their stomachs and provide a good stock for the winter, we will have nine-tenths of the tribe on our side. You can never get all the members to agree on anything. Such is the way of Indian politics. As far as the horses go, I sent the seven men I caught drunk out to find them and haven't heard from them since. I hope they didn't get caught by the Crow.

"You even see it in my small war party," Chaska continued. "We aren't like the White man's army, where the soldiers do whatever the officer says. Our tribe allows people to have a mind of their own and make decisions even if they're unfavorable to the elders or chief, just like Black Mink did with me. Sometimes it costs a man his chiefdom. Nothing is guaranteed when it comes to an Indian tribe. Especially one barely surviving, and so many people are full of discontent. It will all depend on how things work out. We still have to wait and see if Black Mink will try something or not, though it will surprise me if he doesn't."

"Angus, why don't you mosey over to your wife's Crow camp and see if they don't have these men's horses?" Rusty said. "You're the worst shot of the bunch anyway. We'll need 'em to pull the travois to get this meat back to their camp. Make sure your men put that on salt, or it'll go bad with the summer heat."

All the mountain men laughed; strangely enough, even Angus chuckled as Rusty hacked on him. He seemed to hack on everybody at some point, but they all knew it was in fun. They all realized what their strengths and weaknesses were, and they accepted the hard truth. Angus had other attributes to make him necessary. He could shoot well enough to ward off a hostile enemy attack, too. He just wasn't the hunters Rusty, Levi, and Dennis were.

They hadn't ridden a mile from the cabins before Levi saw a large buck elk in the distance. It must have been about a half mile away. Everybody saw it and began to approach with their weapons ready. They heard a shot behind them, and a fraction of a second later, the elk dropped to the ground. Levi acted immediately and didn't give the animal a chance to escape despite the distance. Another one stood behind the first.

"Why that shot must have been over a half mile," Angus snickered, tickled pink. He was enjoying the new blood in the group of older mountain men. They were full of surprises.

A second elk turned to run, and Forrester took a bead, pulled the trigger, and got lucky. He wasn't as good a marksman as Levi by a great deal, but today he felt more confident than usual with the successful negotiation. He hit the buck in the heart, and it, too, dropped beside the first. Both were clean kills.

"There ya go, Chaska." Levi laughed. "Y'all already got two big elk, and we ain't an hour from our cabins. I'd call that a good start."

They hunted the entire morning, and all the mountain men bagged various animals, but Levi got the most because he was a dead shot even from a far distance. Long before the animals smelled them, he managed to put a bullet in them. One of the shots was nearly a mile. Even Rusty Steel, who was a known sharpshooter, marveled at the ease with which the young man took a bead and fired. It was like he wasn't even trying or taking proper aim. It seemed all so natural, like the rifle was an extension of his arm.

"How is it ya shoot so straight?" Rusty asked, curious. "You don't even seem to be trying to hit what you're aiming at. Heck, I hardly see ya aim, boy."

"I don't really know exactly how to explain it," Levi Johnson replied. "I kind of point like when ya point your finger at somethin'. I just know where the chunk of lead is going—as if it was a part of me for a second. My pa said it was a gift I had from when I was a young boy. He noticed it when I was about nine. By the time I was twelve, I was hunting by myself in the dense forests of southeastern Indiana. It was nearly as isolated as here, but there are no mountains."

"Well, if our luck holds, we should have enough meat for these folks in a week," Dennis said. "By Sunday, I'd say we'll be through with everything but makin' the travois, and we've still got to wait on Angus for your horses."

"Why is there so much game here and not where our camp is?" Chaska asked. "We never had this trouble in the past."

"When you trap and hunt, you've first gotta figure how much game is available in your area," Dennis said. "Then ya have to make sure you don't kill more than will be born the following season. The balance of nature is a delicate thing. When you get too greedy or there are too many people to feed in a particular area, you find your streams trapped out and game scarce. You either have to let your game recuperate from all the hunting or look for a better spot for wild game. What we kill this week will affect what we have to hunt during the coming winter and spring. It never fails. That's why the buffalo are so few when they were so many—too many hunters huntin' the same thing in the same stretch of land. The result will end in their extinction.

"Of course, now we have an emergency. But you've got to decide if you live in a place with enough game to survive. Sure, there seems to be plenty of game here right now because we usually put a quota on what we shoot. Angus knows about it because the Crow chief his wife comes from knew how to pick their campsite. It takes more than courage to be a good leader. You've got to think of the simple things, too."

Chaska knew they were right. He had run off half-cocked because he thought the White men were stealing their game. The lack of wild game in so many places showed too many people expected to live off the same game year after year. The same went for their local fishing hole, which was now fished out. Chaska had proposed digging a ditch to a nearby lake so it could replenish, so they'd have fresh fish again by the camp. But if they didn't control what they killed, the same thing would happen again.

That week, they hunted every day until about an hour before sunset. Then they took all the Sioux and gathered their knives, but this time they didn't tie their hands or link them together to avoid escape attempts. It gave them the feeling they were free, which was favorable for their frame of mind. Especially with all the food they had gathered for their starving tribe. Rusty and his friends had allowed them to make camp in the yard before the cabin, where the large campfire roared.

The blood-covered Indians sat before the flames to gather some of the warmth. It came off the orange coals in waves of heat. Cinders shot skyward on thermal currents only to disappear a few yards above the warriors. The sun was just beginning to set on the western horizon, and the men were beaten from six long, hard days of work.

"Do you think we'll finish tomorrow?" Chaska asked.

"Not on Sunday, pilgrim," Rusty said. "We always take the day off on the Sabbath unless we're travelin'. Everybody needs a free day once a week. It honors our religion and gives us a break from the back-breaking work it takes to live up here."

"So you are a religious people?" Chaska asked. "From what religion do you come—Christian?"

"We all be Christians, but that don't mean we go to church and all. There ain't no churches up here," Rusty said. "But livin' here in the mountains, it's impossible not to believe in God. He's all around us everywhere we look. This is God's country, you know. You can see and feel it."

That night, they all knew that with another day of hunting, they would have enough food to get the tribe through the winter. Pete and Sam even threw in a couple of big, thick smoked hams as a treat. They also supplied them with extra coffee and tobacco. As they had had such a good year's sales at the Rendezvous, they had bought more than they thought they would need. Lucky for everybody, they had enough to gift to the Indians, so everybody showed their generosity. It would be a crime to dishonor such benevolence.

That night, when everybody was asleep, Black Mink and two of his friends disappeared. The other two had had a change of heart when they saw how much work the White men put into seeing that their people didn't starve this winter. Their generosity changed their minds about these rugged White men. They understood these were not their enemies and should be grateful for what they had done for them. Chaska had even explained why they were so short on food where they lived, and they all immediately understood. At first, their tribe had been no more than thirty people but now had risen to over a hundred. Next spring, they would have to look for another place to live if they wanted to continue to survive on their own without handouts from White men.

When the mountain men awoke, they found the two warriors that stayed behind sitting in front of the porch waiting for them to wake up. They still slept longer than the Indians. Levi and Bill were the first out the front door.

"Whatcha doin', boys?" they asked with puzzled faces. Chaska came to where they stood with narrowed eyes and frowned. His eyes looked angry. "What's the matter, Chaska?"

"They came to tell you Black Mink and Scalded Dog ran off last night," Chaska said. "Silver Shadow is with them. These wise men decided it would be dishonorable to leave when you are being so generous and feeding our people. Only fools would not see what has been done. Thoughts of glory and songs of the elders cloud Mink's mind. I hope he is smart and returns home, or he will soon find himself a fool on the other side of the spirit world where the dead live."

"You just worry about your men helping us and let the captain and me worry about Black Mink, Scalded Dog, and Silver Shadow," Levi Johnson said. "We know they're there, so with the marksmanship of our men, they won't stand a chance. I still don't know why the fool don't see the painting on the wall."

"He has always been like that, even as a young boy," Chaska said. "We grew up together. He was my neighbor, along with half the warriors. When you live in a small tribe, everybody knows everyone and what they are all doing."

"Whatcha plan to do, Levi?" Rusty asked.

"I plan to track those three scoundrels and see where they're goin'," Levi whispered. "Once I make sure they're headin' back home, we can forget about them and focus on getting these people some more meat. A few wild boar or a couple more elk should do it."

"I'll go with ya," Bill said. "I feel up to it."

"No offense, pard, but I'm much quieter on my own," Levi said. "You're like a wolf in a chicken house when you travel through the woods. A deaf dog could hear ya. Your job is planning things. Just look how you pretty much singlehandedly captured all the warriors. That took some smarts. My specialty is traveling through the woods without making a sound or leaving tracks. You'll just slow me down."

"Make sure you don't end up with an arrow in your back," Chaska warned. "Black Mink is an excellent archer, and Scalding Dog is a fighter. That's how he got the name. Silver Shadow is easy to sway one way or the other. If we deal with the first two, the third one will come on his own.

"Don't get shot for those three fools," Chaska said. "I doubt they will return to our camp, not knowing we solved the food situation; I expect something from

Black Mink. He'll at least have a go at somebody, but I couldn't say when."

"Let me find 'em first, then we'll see how things are gonna go," Levi said just before he turned and disappeared into the woods.

Levi wasn't twenty feet into the vegetation before he vanished. It was like the forest swallowed him up, and he was never there. He was so silent the crickets didn't even stop their chatter.

# MINK-DOG-SHADOW

BLACK MINK AND TWO OF THE FOUR MEN WHO'D VOTED to follow him worked on gutting and skinning the last elk of the day. It was a large animal, so they hung it from a tree by its feet to slit its soft belly open. Then they skinned it and cut the choice pieces of meat from the carcass. Finally, they dropped it to the ground and left the rest for the vultures circling overhead—that and the wolves and coyotes that would show up after dark.

They knew the animals the mountain men killed would go a long way toward filling most of the stomachs of their Sioux camp, especially the children and the elderly. The two men with Black Mink both saw the good the mountain men were doing for them, but the leader was blinded by his desire for glory. It wasn't even about revenge for him because he didn't care about Chaska's brother.

They always had been rivals. He was pleased when he found he had lost his head. It seemed too appropriate for Mink—what better way to close a big mouth than to lop his head off? He got what he deserved because he was a showoff. This made Black Mink jealous. Chaska's brother had been a semi-famous warrior but had never done anything to make songs about. He had hoped the encounter with his White enemy would give him the recognition he sought. All it got him was a ceremony for the dead, so his spirit would pass on to the other side, albeit headless.

"We must wait for a chance to pull two of those fool riders off their horses. We can kill them with our knives and then use their guns to shoot the others. But we'll have to be very fast, or one of us will get shot—maybe even all of us. I would rather die with honor than have to gut filthy animals anyway. We are warriors and shouldn't be forced to do such mundane chores. Our job is to protect and to wage war on our enemies."

"But these people don't act like they're our enemies," Scalded Dog replied. "Why, we aren't even tied up anymore. And lookee over there. War Chief Chaska is helping gut elk, too. He isn't concerned about a warrior's caste or his honor. He's workin' for our people. I think he worries about our starving tribe. Sure, before, he was hypnotized by the possibility of songs made by the elders of his glory. I think he saw the truth and decided to be humble, not a braggart or bully. What are you worrying about, Black Mink? Your reputation? If we fail, we will be disgraced before our people. When they find we have killed the very people who were trying to provide us with food, the chief will become angry, and someone will pay. Have you thought about that?"

"If you like Chaska so much, why don't you join another group to gut these dirty beasts?" Black Mink snarled. "Our job should be killing elk and bear, and White men when possible. They are our sworn enemies. It's a woman's job to clean the carcasses. I won't do women's work."

"They may be your sworn enemy, but my two sons go hungry. This will ensure they will eat all winter. I'll agree with you if you want to flee," Scalded Dog said, "but I don't want to get shot by these White men with guns. You saw them hunt. They never miss and can shoot an animal so far away I can barely see it. They have the scent of a dog, too. I heard from Chaska that they smelled us long before they saw us. What kind of people are these White men?"

"Chaska is a coward," Mink spat. "He's a traitor to our cause and the warrior's code. We are Sioux, and we should be killing White men. That is the natural course of things. That is our destiny."

"I've known Chaska all my life," Silver Shadow said, "and I have never seen him run from a fight. He has always been brave before danger. Maybe what he is doing is braver than we give merit—maybe even braver than you or us."

"Enough with all the nonsense," Mink growled. "I'm the war chief now, and you will do what I say. I will make things easier for you, Scalded Dog. First, we will escape, then we will wait. We know they will take chase. White men always chase poor Indians. These won't be any different. When they all come for us, we will be waiting if we climb tall trees along the trail. We can shoot them with arrows before they even see us. I, too, have plans like the magic back at the White men's cabins. You will see how we all become heroes, and the elders will make songs about what we do. May the spirits be with us."

Two of the men had already abandoned the

wannabe war chief, Mink. There were only three, but still, he believed they could at least kill a couple of White men, if not all of them. When they returned to the camp with blond and brown scalps, they would know who the champions were.

"I hope you're right," Scalded Dog whispered. "If not, we'll all be in a world of trouble."

"No, if not, we will all be dead," Silver Shadow whispered. "These men haven't survived in these mountains for so many years because they are weak, and I am sure we are not the first warriors to try to breach their fences and cabins. Yet they are still here after ten winters. Logic tells me they are very dangerous, or they would not have survived this long. To think otherwise is foolish. I don't want to volunteer for my death."

"First, let's escape. You do want to go free, don't you? Do you trust the White men to let you go and not kill you? I don't trust any White man, no matter who he is and what he knows. Especially mountain men."

He said it like it was a dirty word.

That night the three escaped. The other two refused to go and went to sit before the White man's porch. They would sit there all night and, in the morning, tell the men giving them food what happened. They wished them no harm. They just wanted to help. The escapees moved through the shadows until they reached the edge of the camp and disappeared into the forest. The knives Mink had counted on were taken away after their workday. They said the following day they would be resting. None of the Sioux were left with a weapon. They ran for freedom anyway, even though they were unarmed and on foot.

They ran through the forest toward their camp all night and all the next day.

When they finally stopped, Mink said, "There's no way they will all come this far to find us. If they don't travel at night, it will take them two days to get here. Now we can vanish or wait to see who comes to capture us again. You know they will come. White men always chase people who break their laws."

"Why don't we just go home and forget about all this?" Silver Shadow said. "It is foolish to think we can take these mountain men. I doubt we could kill one, let alone all eight. This is madness, Black Mink. There is no way for us to win."

"Go ahead if you want," Mink snapped as he jumped to anger. He was as angry as a nest of hornets. "I don't need you. And you, Scalded Dog? Do you want to go home, too?"

"No, I don't, but I don't want to die for nothing either," Scalded Dog said. "If I stay with you, I will die for your vanity, and so will Silver Shadow. This you already know but are too hardheaded to see the writing on the wall. This is no longer the war party that we started with. Now, it is a humanitarian joining of people of two races who unite to help those who need and are without."

"Go on, both of you," Black Mink hissed like a snake. "Get out of my sight before I kill you with my bare hands. You're both cowards."

"Perhaps it is better to be a live coward than a dead fool," Silver Shadow said. Then they both turned and continued toward their home and safety.

Black Mink had now lost all reason and was under some grand delusion he alone understood. He felt he alone could conquer the men who lived in a valley they had never even approached before. He seemed obsessed with hampering Chaska's success, even if it didn't seem like a success to him. It was clear to see on his face. He was humble and embarrassed. These were the actions of a weak man, and someone not fit to be a leader.

Mink was so jealous that it was driving him crazy. He knew he should have been the war chief who rode to eradicate the White man in this valley. It was all Chaska's fault that they were captured. Things would not have gotten so out of control if he had been in charge. Chaska had grown soft and weak while Mink had grown hard and strong. It was time he took over as war chief for their small tribe. All he needed was one White man's scalp. He waited for those who would follow to arrive.

He knew he was more intelligent than them all. He only had to prove it somehow. He waited for the enemy with a stick he could use as a club. He hoped only one man was coming to find him, but he knew there would be more. Still, he couldn't consider any other course of action. He had committed himself to this one hundred percent.

———

LEVI JOHNSON HAD no trouble at all following the warriors' tracks. They were making no effort to disguise where they were going. He could only assume they were waiting to bushwhack him when he wasn't expecting it. He was almost sure they didn't have any knives. Captain Forrester had personally disarmed the captives for the next day because it was Sunday. Nobody in the compound worked on Sunday. He wasn't sure if it was a religious thing or if they just wanted one day a week off work like most folks.

Since he already suspected what they were up to, he swung wide to arrive somewhere in front of them. He raced through the forest, appearing occasionally as not much more than a blur as he sped by. He could run like that all day long and all night for two days. He had done it before. They didn't make them any harder than Levi Johnson. His long legs covered twice the ground of a small man, and his muscles never seemed to tire. He had been running in the wilderness since he was a young boy. It was in his blood.

Soon, he would be waiting to ambush the Sioux warriors. He still didn't have an exact plan. It depended on what they did. If they were unarmed and gave themselves up, he would accept their surrender, but if they put up a fight, he would have to wing it and change his course as he went. Levi was looking for a place where five warriors could hide to ambush him. He knew it didn't have to be big, but it would have to be bigger than a rock or a bush. With a small cover, five men couldn't remain out of sight in such numbers. He raced forward as fast as a man dared in such a situation. He had to move twice as quickly as they did to catch up and set his own trap.

Suddenly, he noticed a familiar scent in the air. It was the aftershave the captain insisted on wearing, even though Levi had warned him. He was distracted for a moment as he shot a glance back over his shoulder, looking for some sign of Forrester. Levi had told him not to follow, but his scent told him he'd come anyway. When he looked back, it was too late.

———

CAPTAIN BILL FORRESTER wasn't about to let his closest friend Levi Johnson run off on his own with five dangerous warriors running free and probably looking to kill a White man or two. He rode forward with abandon. He felt that everybody who would want to know where he was already knew, so he rode his white stallion fast, throwing caution to the wind.

He knew he must be close. He listened for something, but he heard nothing. Then he remembered how quietly Levi traveled. That was when he saw his friend on the trail before him. Bill put the reins between his teeth and pulled his saber.

Black Mink came out of nowhere and swung his club, hitting Levi square on the forehead. He saw stars and toppled over. It happened so fast, and his mind was so fuzzy from the blow, he couldn't recuperate in time to stop the Sioux warrior from getting on top of him. Somehow, he got Levi's knife out of his boot, and he drew it back to stab the hot steel to the hilt into the White man's heart. The sun flashed off the blade as it shined in his eyes. It happened so fast that he wasn't sure if he was dead or alive.

Levi startled as blood splatter hit his face. Mink blinked his eyes in surprise. He stared at where his arm and hand had been a second before. He looked on the ground and saw it laying there. He picked it up with jerky, clumsy movements and tried to put it back on, but it fell to the ground again. The blood drained from his face, and it turned an ashen gray. It was the color of death, but Mink wasn't meant to die just yet.

Forrester pulled off Mink's belt, wrapped it around his stump, and said, "Pull that tight, so you don't bleed to death. We're too far from the cabins to do it there, so we'll have to tend to it here. Will ya make me a fire while I hold on to the tourniquet, Levi? He looks like he might pass out on me at any minute."

"He deserves to die," Forrester spat. "He had no call to try to kill you. I should have taken off his head like I did Chaska's brother."

"It was just as well ya didn't," Levi said. "Loppin' off heads seems to rile the local Indians up something fierce. It's best he's left to live. Now, he'll have to go through what you went through. Now, we'll see how much of a man he is."

Levi looked at the Indian and yelled, "Now you're gonna feel what it's like to have to do everything with your left hand!" He turned to Bill and asked, "He is right-handed, ain't he? Oh, it don't matter, because he can't understand me anyhow."

"Something tells me he's getting the point." Forrester chuckled.

# FOOD FOR THE HUNGRY

WHEN LEVI AND FORRESTER RODE INTO THE SIOUX CAMP, the women and children ran for their lives at first sight of them. Chaska took the lead, so the warriors knew they were with him, and everyone was to stand down. There was a specific protocol to follow in the stronghold. The chief of the tribe had to be informed first. Both men looked strange to the Indians, especially the captain, who had what they called yellow-hair. Some even dared to touch it when he allowed it. It was soft to the touch and the color of the sun.

Behind Captain Forrester walked Black Mink. He had his single wrist tied, and a rope ran from his hand to Bill's saddle horn. He dragged his heels as he struggled to keep up with the horses. He would be ridiculed for what he did as soon as the warriors and hunters told the tribe. Neither Levi nor the captain had any urge to have anybody suffer anymore. The captain had shed blood yet again, but at least he didn't have to kill him. But like Forrester, his life would now be changed forever.

Time would tell if he came to terms with the loss of an arm or would become a tribe beggar. Now was the real test of his mettle. Everything before now was minor compared to facing his chief for betraying his tribe. He wished this man Beaver had killed him. Anything would have been better than losing his arm. How would he tie his moccasins and shoot a bow? Sweat glistened on his face as half moons showed under his arms. His mouth was no more than a gash as he fought through the pain without a whimper. At least he intended to show them he was still a proud warrior even if he had failed miserably, gone off directionless, and made more of a mess of things than made any wrongs right.

First came Chaska as he pulled to a stop before the chief's lodge. Then Levi and Forrester pulled up beside the war chief. There was clearly no animosity between the mounted men.

After them came to Black Mink and finally, eight horses and eight mules pulling travois full of food. The other Sioux warriors never showed with the horses Levi ran off. Green Leaves said they weren't in the Sioux camp. Time would tell if the braves and the horses ever showed up. Stacks of meat were piled high on each travois. They would have a feast tonight. The tribe's mouths watered as they imagined the smell of fresh meat on the grill. Everybody was starving.

A dozen women immediately prepared fires and spits to roast the meat, and water with lemon to refresh their parched throats. The camp went from a sluggish existence to instant activity. Everybody knew exactly what to do. When the chief came out, he could see mountains of meat for his hungry people. He looked from one White man to the other with a puzzled face. Chaska couldn't help but laugh.

It had turned out better than he had ever imagined. He had received a lesson in humility and learned to be humble before his fellow man. He had learned more on this journey than in his entire life. Maybe one day, he would be chief after all. Now, he saw the way was through wisdom, and everything else follows.

When the tribe saw all the animals with travois full of food, tobacco, and coffee, they all got excited. Chaska had brought them badly needed nourishment. It appeared that the White men helped him. When they looked at Black Mink, they all wondered what he had done to be dragged by a rope. Soon, the whole story would be out, and everybody would know who was a coward and who was a fool.

The tribe had plenty of food for the rest of the summer and the coming winter. When Levi and Bill rode out of the camp, they had a tingly feeling that went from the top of their heads to their toes. It was how you felt when you did something good for humankind. They'd helped their fellow man and survived yet another season. Not because they were selfish but because they were generous and kind to those in need.

# BUFFALO

## LEVI JOHNSON MOUNTAIN MAN SCOUT 4

*This book is dedicated to those who lost their lives on the flight to Pokhara, Nepal.*

*01/16/23*

"I do not fear death. I had been dead for billions and billions of years before I was born and had not suffered the slightest inconvenience from it."

**Mark Twain**

# RUSTLED HORSES

WHEN THE SIOUX INDIAN DARK HORSE MOVED FORWARD into the forest, it was easy to follow the rustled horses. They still didn't know if it was Ute, Blackfeet, or Crow, although they were told they had a camp located a half day's ride from the mountain men's cabins. They just weren't sure in which direction. What they were certain of was that they were traveling in enemy territory. He and the six other braves who War Chief Chaska had caught with whiskey—the White men's spirits—carefully tiptoed through the wilderness, knowing they could be coming closer to one of their sworn enemies with every step.

They carefully picked their way through the night, undetected with the full moon. They moved from shadow to shadow to avoid being seen if enemy spies were out. They could see where the man had dismounted. He must have spooked the horses for them to continue running when he abandoned them—but why? Even in the silvery moonlight, it was plain to see. They still didn't know from what tribe the thief might be and why he abandoned the horses and ran back to where he came from on foot.

Dark Horse suddenly realized it wasn't Indians who had stolen their horses. The mountain men had spirited them off in the night when Dark Horse was drunk on the White man's whiskey. That was what put him to sleep. He had never tried drinking spirits before. He doubted he ever would again. Especially with how he and his six friends felt the next day as they trudged through the wilderness with their heads splitting and their hearts hammering between their ears. The group of seven all felt nauseous and off balance. It was as though they had been poisoned. With as much as they drank, they might have been.

As far as he could tell, it was a single man responsible for them losing all the horses. How could that be? Even an Indian couldn't achieve such a feat. Looking back on what had happened, he still found it hard to believe a lone thief could have run off all the horses without some help. If his war party had to do the same, it would take half a dozen men to do what one mountain man achieved. Who were these strange people?

The warrior remembered back to what War Chief Chaska had said when he caught them drunk and the horses missing. *If you don't come back with the horses, you aren't welcome to return.* Only if they regained their honor would they be allowed to come back to live with the small Sioux tribe. Dark Horse's wife was back in the village with his infant son. He knew he had to find the horses even if he died trying. He didn't want to live in some other tribe without his family.

Dark Horse should have known straight away that the horses weren't stolen by the Crow, Ute, or even

Blackfeet. They were no more than a small herd of nags and worn-out horses with lungs that sounded like steam engines. They didn't even have enough meat on their bones to entice another tribe to eat them, but still, they were the only horses the poor Sioux had. Now, he had to find them and return home, no matter the risks or their actual value.

It was now about honor and not animals. They had to complete the task or forsake their families and be outcasts forever. When a chief makes such a declaration, there is no taking it back unless another, even greater, feat is achieved. Dark Horse felt they would be lucky if they found their herd of scraggly horses. That itself seemed like they were going to have to climb a mountain. He could do that or abandon his family, but he loved them too much. He would prefer to give up his life trying.

They trotted through the woods as the first signs of a new day filtered through the tree trunks, branches, and leaves. A morning breeze came with the sun, making the branches sway and leaves break loose and fly through the air. It was the very first sign of the coming of winter. They all had a keen sense of smell and knew they had to turn around and run for their lives if they smelled smoke. That would indicate they had come too close to the Crow village, wherever it was. This was a constant worry for the warriors.

Coyote squatted and looked at the tracks. They veered sharply to the left and back toward the cabins. As they followed the hoofprints, they did so with deep sighs of relief. Some of the nervousness of traveling through an unknown forest peeled away like the skin of an onion—one layer at a time. Soon they were trotting along, no longer worried about the Crow camp because now they were traveling in the opposite direction. Heading back toward the mountain men's cabins seemed safer. It wasn't exactly the way they came, but they were heading in the same general direction.

Dark Horse wondered how the attack on the White men's camp went. War Chief Chaska was a brave leader, but they still needed a wagonload of luck. It was one thing catching mountain men on the trail, but it was another attacking cabins that were built more like small forts to ward off any type of intruder—Indians and wild beasts included. At the moment, all they could do was follow the tracks and go wherever they led them, even if it was to their deaths.

"Wait," Coyote whispered. He squatted, pushed his long black hair over his shoulder, and felt the form of the new prints with his fingers. "These are shod horses and not Indian ponies. Whoever they are, they have taken the herd of horses. They will be White men, but there are only three, and we are seven. I believe somebody else has found our horses. Now, we are going back the way we came."

"Maybe they were with the man who stole the horses. I knew there had to be more rustlers. They have guns, and we only have our bows and arrows," Rain Man said. He wore three eagle feathers in his hair and hawk claws through his earlobes. "With such dense forest, it will be easy to sneak up on them. We can kill the three White men when we get close enough and head home with the horses."

Of course, if you found thirty horses running around the mountain with nobody tending them, the obvious thing to do was take them. Nobody lets horses they want roam around loose. Usually, in such a case, the owner was dead. Also, in most cases, finders keepers. Unfortunately for the seven Sioux, these had owners, and they were responsible for them, so they would have to follow. Without the horses, Chaska and his men wouldn't allow them back into the camp.

Dark Horse felt his luck had been going downhill quickly since Chaska decided to form a war party and go on this raid. The first night, everything had gone wrong. He wondered if his luck had improved, or if they would encounter more disasters. Maybe these men were cleverer than they had believed. Time would tell.

Now that they were headed in a safe direction, they abandoned their stealth and ran through the woods without fear. They knew they were getting close. Maybe their luck was changing. At least now their horses wouldn't be in a Crow camp, a place they would surely lose their lives if they attempted to steal them back. But with three White men, things had changed for the better. They now had superior numbers, and the men with the horses didn't know a Sioux war party was following them.

They had low esteem for the trespassers that came to the Rocky Mountains to hunt buffalo and trap their beavers. Especially those that hunted their bison, which had dramatically dropped in numbers over the last few years. Now, they had to search for days and sometimes weeks to find smaller herds scattered across the plains. Long gone were the herds that stretched from horizon to horizon like the elders' songs told in their tales. The White men had said there were sixty million buffalo on the plains before the hunters came. As they arrived in hordes to kill them, encouraged by the US Army, the animals' numbers dropped dramatically yearly. A starving tribe was easier to defeat.

Some places on the Great Plains had mountains of buffalo bones stacked as high as three-story buildings. These would later be gathered and shipped back East to sell as fertilizer. Others would be used to make domestic objects like buttons, corset stays, crochet hooks, and even umbrella handles.

Coyote was their point man and tracker. He could track a water moccasin across a river without losing the trail. He also had a keen sense of smell, which was essential for a warrior running out in front of his support team. He was there to spot danger and, if necessary, to draw fire if they were attacked. This would give the main party time to repel whatever trouble was waiting.

When Coyote squatted again, the war party acted in kind. They held their hands over the horses' mouths to muffle the sound if they nickered. Nobody moved a muscle as their guide and tracker smelled for any foreign odors: White men's soap, sweat, or even rose oil. But instead, he smelled the faintest scent of fire. The smell of smoke was distant, but when he separated the other odors, it stood out strongly.

Coyote sniffed again and whispered, "It's only one campfire and not a big Crow camp. We must be nearing the rustlers."

He shot a glance over his shoulder at Dark Horse and said, "I think we have found them. They are still a good distance away, so we don't have to worry yet." He closed his eyes and took a deep breath of air. "They are cooking meat too." His stomach grumbled at the thought of a thick steak.

"If they are White men, we will take the horses back at night when they are asleep," Rain Man said.

"We can do the same thing the mountain men did to us," Raven added. "That would be the appropriate revenge, and we would show them that we are as skilled as them."

"I smell something else," Dark Horse warned. "I smell buffalo hides. I should have smelled them before now, but we were upwind. Now, it's shifted; it stinks."

"Buffalo hunters have bad reputations," Rain Man said. "I have heard they kill Indians when they find them hunting a herd they want. They shoot them from a great distance like they do the bison. We must be careful and approach them only at night, or we might get shot. Then we'll never get home."

"Would you rather be banished from the tribe?" Dark Horse asked. "All you have to do is walk away. I won't stop you. I intend to return home with the horses. I don't know how yet, but I must."

"If we stay here and talk all day, they're going to die of old age before we reach them," Man Who Runs said. "I want to go home, too, so go on if you don't want to see your family, Rain Man."

"I'm not married like you, and I don't have a son or daughter," Rain Man said. "I am going to try to find my cousin's Crow camp. Maybe I will be welcome there."

"I'm going with you," Leopard said. "I have a wife, but she has grown sour, and I would rather not see her again. It will be safer if we travel together."

"May the spirits protect you both," Dark Horse said. He smiled at his friends, and it reached his eyes.

Both men turned and disappeared into the forest.

"We are still five, and they are only three," Dark

Horse said after a moment of silence. Nobody expected to lose two of their warriors, but it was true: Rain Man had no family, and Leopard's wife was famous for her fury. Dark Horse stifled a chuckle as he thought of how angry she would be when he didn't return.

"We're not getting any closer standing here," Dark Horse said. "I'll take the point, and Chato, you ride drag. We must make sure we don't stumble on a guard or get attacked from behind."

They tied their horses back in a gully where they couldn't be seen from the trail. They tied and hobbled them, hoping they would be there when they returned. They hadn't had much luck with horses lately. All five men began to move forward again. They had their quivers full of arrows and their bows in one hand. The other they kept free to throw a lance, knife, or tomahawk.

It was cool out but just the same, their buckskin shirts stuck to their sweaty backs. Their faces glistened with sweat. Their hearts raced in their chests. Dark Horse set a pace, and he ran at a trot. They moved through the forest, hardly making a sound. They stopped for several minutes every half hour to listen and smell their environment. The smell of smoke grew more assertive.

"We better wait until dark before we close in on the buffalo hunters and the horses," Dark Horse whispered. "We have to make sure they're asleep. If we're lucky, they will be drunk like the White men at the Rendezvous."

"You saw how much whiskey they could drink. It made them wild, but I didn't see many falls. The liquor doesn't seem to affect them like it does us," Chato said.

"We drank little compared to them, and it made me sleep and later gave me a bad headache. I still feel sick."

"They say the buffalo hunters can kill a man from all the way across a valley," Dark Horse said. "We better find some dense brush to hide in. Then we can sleep in turns and then move again at night. We are close to the enemy, so we have to be careful. We all want to go home again, so we can't make any mistakes."

It was still daylight, and they didn't want to give the buffalo hunters a target to shoot at. So, they found some dense brush and crawled in. They took turns sleeping and watching for any movement or any sign of danger at all. They were all nervous, but they were so weary they all fell into a deep sleep. Even Dark Horse, who was supposed to be on watch, dozed off and on. They were exhausted. The leaves on the bush kept them in the shade from the overhead sun and rustled in the breeze.

# BEAR CLAWS

"WHATCHA DOIN', PARD?" PLAINSMAN BILL FORRESTER asked as he stepped out the door of Rusty's cabin and onto the porch. The bright sun shined down on the little compound.

"Do you remember them bear claws I chopped off the paws of the critter we killed?" Levi asked. "I've got another set for me, and I'm makin' us necklaces. To tell the truth, I was embarrassed to wear 'em before Rusty and the boys considered us mountain men. I didn't want to brag when all we did was kill a couple of grizzlies. Now, I believe it's time to show off a little. You've seen how Angus wears all kinds of Crow doodads, and Rusty himself wears a necklace of mountain lion claws and a bracelet with two canine bear teeth. It must have been a monster considerin' their size."

"Why, thank you, Levi," Bill replied. "Let me try it on. I've only seen the odd mountain man and Indian wearing bear claws this big." Then Levi showed him his. "Dang, that must have been a heck of a big bear to have claws that size, and here I thought mine were special."

Levi pushed his necklace under his buckskin shirt. He didn't want to show off too much since they had just been accepted into this tribe of White men living in the Indian territories. They were finally living the life that legends were made of.

"One thing I did do is throw that bottle of fancy aftershave away," Bill said. "You know that stuff you smelled when the Sioux warrior attacked? I believe it was because you smelled the rose oil that made you turn around and right where the bugger was sitting, waiting to clobber you on the head. I believe it's better to smell like bear claws than aftershave. At least here in the wilderness. Were we back in civilization, I like the smell of rose oil over that of sweat."

"If you hadn't saved me and lopped his arm off, I'd be dead today," Levi said. "So, how was it your fault?"

"If I hadn't been following, you would have known he was there," Bill replied. "Instead, you smelled me coming up behind you. I don't believe for a minute that you would have missed him. That good sense of smell business can work either way, though. I believe smelling me drew your attention off your target. It was just unlucky; the scoundrel was right there waiting. You've got a knot on your head the size of an egg."

The young mountain man pulled out a towel and some lye soap and walked over to the mirror hanging on the porch wall. He eyed his fractured reflection as he fingered the walnut-sized bump on his forehead. His thick uncombed head of brown hair and beard and his bronzed olive skin looked distorted in the looking glass. His eyes were so dark they almost looked black. He grabbed a wash-up pan, filled it with water, sat it on a barrel, and began washing his hands and face.

"You aren't using smelly soap, are you?" Bill asked and laughed. "The next time we go hunting, we can scare up a skunk first. Then we'll have a smell that'll turn the bravest warrior around and running the other way."

"That's not a bad idea for a dangerous situation." Levi chuckled. "Have ya ever been sprayed by a skunk? It takes a week for the smell to disappear, and it stinks somethin' fierce."

"I've smelled them often enough but never had the misfortune to be sprayed by one," Bill Forrester said. "It is a rather unpleasant smell, but it would probably work just the same. When I smell a skunk, I turn and run the other way."

Rusty was sitting on the porch on a chair tilted up against the side of the building. The last chips of green paint from years ago was peeling off the wall. He was carving on a wood block, attempting to turn it into a horse. He looked up when Levi walked out, and his eyes danced with mischief. He pulled on his graying beard and grinned.

"Now that we've hunted for the Sioux Indians' winter food stock, I reckon we better be headin' out to hunt for our vittles for the winter," Rusty said. "It won't be long before it starts to get cold during the day. The nights are already cool to cold on an occasional evening. At least you got all the firewood cut, Levi."

"I promised Dennis I would help him with his, too," Levi said. "It won't take me but a couple of days."

"You're more valuable with me hunting elk, deer, and bear, son," Rusty said. "We can chop wood even after a light snow, but the hunting can't be put off any longer. What if we have to ride a long distance to find the meat we need? We've killed a passel of critters for that Sioux tribe. I know they were starvin' and all, but we might have shot ourselves in the foot.

"It's much harder going in the winter, plus we'll be busy with the beaver traps and hides. Every time of year has its chores. Once we're done with our work, we can tend to Dennis. He's just lazy, is all. He's like Angus. If you tell him to cut wood, he'll just run off to his Crow wife's camp and disappear for a week or two. There ain't nothing he hates more than swingin' an axe."

"I kind of like it," Levi smiled. "All that exercise gets my blood flowin'."

"If I were as big as you, I'd probably like it too." Rusty chuckled. "For you, it's like whittling toothpicks. How tall are ya anyway, Levi?"

"Last I checked, I'm six feet seven and weighed some two hundred pounds, but that was a year ago. I've filled out some since, but I doubt I've grown anymore."

"If ya fill out anymore, you won't fit through the front door." Rusty laughed. He seemed to spend a lot of his time chuckling or laughing at the things others did. He appeared entertained with the smallest detail and used everyday life as his stage, like a theater with an audience of one. "I reckon you boys better go get some more game or you're gonna eat us out of house and home this winter."

"When do you want us to start hunting?" Levi asked. He immediately got the young frontiersman's interest. There was nothing he liked to do more than hunting and trapping critters.

"If you and I ride out front with Dennis, the other four can gut and skin the animals, then pack the meat on the mules." Rusty Steel smiled. "Being a good shot with a rifle comes with its perks, pard. It means we three don't end up with blood up to our armpits. Two or three buffs, and we'll be done. If there ain't no buffalo, we'll hunt for adult elk. They have the most meat and will be easier to find. We wanna make sure we don't kill any young animals, though. The younger animals will be for next year or the year after once they've dropped a foal or two. We just don't want any more surprises after that scrape with the Sioux.

"We got clever and lucky and didn't get a scratch and captured the Indians without a shot. I reckon that's a first for us. Most of that was due to Levi here and Forrester. We can leave Angus behind to keep an eye on his horse and the cabins. Green Leaf is with him, so we'll have plenty of eyes on the rest. We'll need his mule to carry meat if we get lucky and run into a small herd of buffalo. If he sees trouble brewin', he'll send us an alarm."

"If he shoots off a gun, we'll hear him unless we're too far away," Levi said. "What then? We're bound to go out of range of a pistol or rifle shot. Or even a double blast from a shotgun."

"He'll light a stick of dynamite and throw it at whoever it is he's trying to run off." Rusty laughed. "We'll hear a blast like that from miles away, boy. We've always got some explosives around to remove the big tree stumps."

"Why don't this place of y'all's have a name?" Levi asked. The question seemed to surprise Rusty and left him lost for words.

"To be honest, you're the first person that suggested it," Rusty replied. His eyes narrowed as he thought. "I wonder why we've never thought of such a thing. We've always called it home before."

"I figure such a special place should have a special name," Levi said. Now it was his turn to laugh. It was rare that they caught Rusty Steel off guard.

"The next time we're all on the porch, and nothing's happening, remind me," Rusty said. "I wonder what Dennis and the other boys got to say about that. I'm surprised we've made such an oversight."

"I wonder if the Crow have a name for it?" Levi asked.

"Iffin they do, it probably won't be kindly," Rusty said. "I still don't know why they let Angus come and go as he pleases. That McFarlin is a rare bird, he is."

The following morning, seven men headed out on horseback with eight mules trailing them. Angus stood at the edge of the porch and watched them disappear on the trail leading higher into the mountains. Three of the riders galloped on ahead until they had a good lead on the others, then they bumped their horses down to a trot. They began to spy on the woods and the horizon for signs of wild game. At the same time, they searched for trails of smoke, unusual sounds, and dangerous odors. Dennis stopped every little bit to take a whiff of his surroundings.

Rusty nudged his horse with his spurs, and he rode on ahead. Dennis and Levi struggled to keep up. If you didn't keep sharp, Rusty would disappear on you when you least expected. He was as crafty as a Comanche when it came to sneaking around. They rode on for half a day before they saw two white-tailed deer on a distant ridge. They were pulling at tufts of grass, oblivious to the danger some seven hundred yards away.

Levi raised his rifle and looked over at Rusty. He nodded, giving the signal. Both shots seemed simultaneous. Gray smoke blurred their vision for a moment. On the ground across the gorge lay two dead animals. A spray of red covered the trees behind them.

Rusty wheeled his horse around and gigged it toward Pete, Sam, Bob, and Forester. When he got in shouting range, he yelled, "You've got some work to do, boys. Over yonder, you'll find two deer on the top of that ridge. They ain't that big, but they'll be mighty fine eatin'." He laughed some more. "I love to see you boys doin' a hard day's work. There ain't nothin' I like better than watching y'all tend to the heavy chores. Thank God I was born a dead shot."

"It's about time we found something," Sam retorted. "I figured you'd lost your knack."

"The problem is we hunted out the area around our cabins to help out the Sioux," Syracuse Sam complained.

Since a Blackfoot warrior scalped him some years back, he'd never trusted an Indian again. He was lucky to have survived the ordeal. The group consisted of a good variety of characters. Of course, Dennis and Rusty sort of steered things in the right direction without seeming like somebody's boss or captain. After Rusty lost his men to pirates, he didn't want to be in charge of anyone else. Angus was the last man on earth you would pick for a woman's man. Bob twisted his long gray mustache with his fingers. The tips were covered in wax.

"You should have bagged five or six animals by now," Pete added. His hazel eyes were as big as a doe. He would have been good-looking if it weren't for the pockmarks. "If you lollygag around here all day jawin', I doubt you'll kill any more than a couple of tame rabbits."

Pete was the sole survivor of a family of thirteen after smallpox hit the town where they lived. The few townsfolks that did survive ran away for fear they, too, would die. Some unknowingly took the sickness with them. That pushed Portland Pete to the mountains and away from the cities and dense populations. Lucky for the mountain men, Pete didn't bring smallpox with him.

Each had a unique story, their different reasons for abandoning everything and living in the wilderness—everybody but Levi Beaver Johnson. He had lived his entire life in the wilderness, minus the mountain peaks and grizzly bears. He came to the mountains because he could hear them calling. He wasn't running away from anything. He was running full steam ahead toward his destiny.

Unlike his friend, Forrester, who was running away from failure in the face of his peers. That and the loss of so many men when their expedition tried to cross Kansas. They all had a story, except Levi. Maybe that was why he was one the best woodsman of them all, and he was still learning hand over fist. No one doubted his skills would eclipse that of all the others in a year.

"The forest used to be teeming with wild game, but now it appears our part of the woods is getting over-hunted too," Bob said.

"It'll be all right again next year," Rusty replied. "We just have to travel farther to find what we need, just like the Sioux when they came to our hunting grounds. It looks like it's the same all over."

Rusty wheeled his horse Spirit toward the other two

hunters. He raced all the way there and then slid to such an abrupt stop his horse nearly sat down. He could ride almost as well as a Comanche. There were more things for Levi to learn from him.

"Now they've got something to do other than lollygag behind us, we can head deeper into the mountains." Rusty grinned. "There ain't nothing but Crow on this side, and they be peaceful with us. At least until now. Then again, you just never know. All it takes is for one White man to make trouble, and they'll turn against us all. It's always been that way with the Indians."

He believed it was the same with White men. One rogue war party broke off and killed a few settlers, and the army went berserk and killed every Indian they could find, even if they were from different tribes. Most military men couldn't tell a Sioux from a Comanche.

"Come on now," Rusty said just before he gigged Spirit into a comfortable trot. "Let's go find us something bigger to hunt. Maybe we can get lucky and scare up a grizzly bear. Then we'll have both meat and a new coat for this winter."

Levi and Dennis wheeled their horses around and followed their witty friend. He probably wasn't over forty-five, but he seemed pretty old to the newcomers. Then again, they were just in their twenties. For them, anybody over forty was an old man.

Levi was glad he was such a good shot. He loved to go hunting and would do it every chance he had, even when he wasn't told to. He had enjoyed it since his childhood. He remembered back to the mountain lion that intended to have him for lunch back when he was a kid. It chased him all the way home and even across a lake. The mankiller was found and shot the next day. The reign of terror was over.

Now, they were on the hunt for large elk, mountain lions, or grizzly bears. Even the odd moose would do in a pinch. They weren't picky about what they ate. With the new chicken coop, they had fresh eggs, too. Considering where they lived, they ate like kings. At least, they usually did. If they didn't scare up a passel of meat for the coming winter, they would have to ration. Now, there were eight of them to feed.

Good meals, furs to cure, and time to repair broken weapons or tools was done in February, when the weather was too hostile to move farther from the compound than the outhouse. That was guaranteed a cold experience even for the hardiest mountain man. When a bare butt made contact with a freezing wooden seat, it sent goosebumps across the body and could even make your teeth chatter. It turned some of the bravest men into whimpering whiners. And if you had to linger, you risked having bits and pieces get frostbite, something everyone made sure they avoided.

Lucky for the three groups of men, their cabins were well-built and prepared for all weather. Inside each house were giant fireplaces at the front and a smaller chimney for cooking in the far back corner near a window. It provided light for the kitchen and aired out the house in the summer months after making up a meal. The cabins were nearly identical except for the porches. Rusty's was four times bigger than the other two. He loved his nights chewing the fat on the porch or just something as simple as smoking his pipe.

Forrester even decided the cabin folks needed an outdoor shower. During the winter, the weather made washing your face and hands a big deal, with the cold but during the summer with the sun shining down, he knew he could use it to heat the water. He and Levi made short work of a long job. They used rope to pull two barrels onto the roof of the lowest part of the barn. Then they pulled buckets of water to the top and poured them into the barrels. While Johnson was busy securing the barrels, Forrester hooked up some water pipes from the shed and had a shower in no time.

Half the men thought it was a waste of time, but Bill and Levi used it every afternoon. They showered in sun-warmed water fresh from the spring near the compound.

# BUFFALO HUNTERS

THE CLOPPING OF HORSES' HOOVES COULD BE HEARD IN the distance. A cloud of summer dust corkscrewed behind more than thirty horses. They whinnied and snorted as they trotted. Three buckskin-clad men drove the livestock. If they kept riding like they were, they would probably see the mountain men's cabins soon, although they were oblivious to their existence. They had just come off the plains from shooting buffalo with long rifles from a safe distance.

Generally, they were no more than turkey shoots. They would plug away at the poor dumb animals all day long as others removed the hides, leaving hundreds of carcasses to rot in the sun. By the end of the day, there would be massive dead beasts by the hundreds across the valley—and all within a Hawken rifle's shooting range. Some said with the right shooter, that could be up to as much as a mile.

Their red carcasses contrasted with the brown hairy animals grazing at their feet—for some unknown reason, they were drawn to the dead animals. They were too dumb to run unless something spooked them. Then they would move as one solid mass of animals, destroying everything in their path. The buffalo hunters worked from a safe platform above the giant herds. They located elevated shooting positions to ensure they weren't on the valley floor if the herd got scared and ran.

Now, they were hunting for meat to make it down the mountain before winter set in. They believed that with a good feed all winter, the horses they'd found would fetch a few dollars even if they were in rough shape. No matter how much they tried to understand, they couldn't figure out why Indians would leave horses to run loose for any finder that might happen by. At first, they were a little paranoid. Maybe the hostiles were nearby, and the horses were bait, but after hours of riding, they knew they had been abandoned, although nobody had a clue of why.

"These horses are such nags they're slowin' us down," Elroy Grimms spat. "I say we cut the worst ones out of the herd and let 'em fend for themselves. The rest we can take down the mountain. Just because you find something free doesn't mean it's worth keepin'."

"If we're gonna take fifteen, we might as well take the thirty if they can make it," Ely Grimms replied. "We can always sell 'em to make soap. I don't see no sense in throwing money away."

"Even if they're only worth a few dollars, it all adds up," brother Earnest said. "Our buffalo expedition wasn't nearly as good as last year's. We've got half the hides we had last season. That's not a good sign, boys. I figure a few dollars from some free horses will go a long way to help make up the difference."

When the Grimms brothers' ran across the horses,

they had just finished their buffalo hunting trip. This year, they'd had to ride twice as far to find a sizable herd. Now, the buffalo weren't seen from one horizon to another anymore. Now, they were more scattered herds of more manageable sizes. The masses of millions of bison of yesteryear seemed to be suddenly slipping away. Nobody knew how many hunters there were, but they had to be in the hundreds, if not thousands. The buffalo's huge carcasses were left to decay and rot, and their bleached bones were strewn across the deserts and the lonely plains as far as the eye could see.

Part of a government scheme was to eradicate the buffalo, leaving the Plains Indians without a source of food, clothing, homes, and tools. Many nomadic tribes followed the herds to survive. The plan was to force the Indians to find other means of living, like growing crops. They felt this would cause the Native Americans to cultivate a friendship with or reliance on White men. Washington felt when the buffalo were all gone, the government would control the land and the Indian tribes.

Commercial hunters emerged from all parts of the globe—from California, New York, and as far away as Europe. Even the US Army sanctioned and endorsed the wholesale slaughter of the herds of buffalo. This was done primarily to pressure the Native Americans onto the Indian reservations. What better way to win a battle without a shot fired? Instead, they removed their food source.

They planned to force the Indians to leave the plains and move onto reservations or starve to death on the very ground they and their forefathers had hunted for the last ten thousand years. White American Europeans had changed that in just a few years. The herds had gone from sixty million to just a few million in a short span of time.

"From the looks of things, there ain't all that much to hunt around here either," Ely said, using the flat of his hand to shade his eyes as he squinted into the distance. He scoured the horizon and mountains until his eye caught sight of something.

Then he pointed his finger and said, "Lookee over there. Right in front of us stands a buck elk. You boys stay here and watch the horses. I'll be back as soon as I kill and butcher that critter. Get a fire ready, brothers. We'll be feasting tonight."

Ely dropped off his horse, stuck his finger in his mouth, and held it up as he did a three-sixty. He pulled a tuft of grass and dropped it to the ground. The breeze was crossways, and he wanted to stay downwind. He had another look at his target and then instantly disappeared into the forest. Ely Grimms was the eldest of the brothers. They all shared red hair, freckles, and noses as flat as shoes. The brothers were tall and gangly, but they knew what they were doing in the wilderness. Anyone who had spent a few years hunting bison had to be as rugged as they come.

As often as not, some Indian tribe was interested in the same herds as the white and black hunters, so it was dangerous business, not to mention the stampedes. Like the woods and mountains, the plains had inherent dangers of which one had to beware.

Ely took a bead and eased the pressure on the hair trigger. The gun fired, and a flame gushed from the end of the barrel as the chunk of lead hit the target, and gun smoke lingered in the air. The elk dropped to its knees,

but it was a bad shot. It staggered to its feet as Ely
rushed for the wounded creature while reloading on the
run. It staggered over the rise in the land and disappeared behind the hill. The Grimms elder pulled the
hammer back again as he followed his rifle barrel over
the hillside. A giant elk with a full rack could do some
severe damage if it caught you by surprise, especially if
it was wounded and felt cornered and was fighting for
its life.

The shot wasn't as bad as Ely thought. The elk lay
dying just over the rise. It was a monster and had
resisted with every ounce of strength it had. But its
heart stopped; that was all she wrote. Ely roped its hind
legs, used his horse to drag it to a tree, and lifted it off
the ground so he could gut and skin the animal. Two
hours later, he was covered in blood, but he had a stack
of steaks on the back of the mule.

He mounted up and turned for his waiting brothers.
As soon as he rode over the hill, he could see the trail of
smoke snake into the sky in the distance. They had the
fire ready. He could almost smell the sizzling steaks over
hot coals. His belly grumbled. Behind him, high in the
sky, vultures circled the recently killed carcass. Several
descended in a dive before the wolves and coyotes
arrived. Crows had already lined up on the branches
closest to the dead animal. Soon, a swarm of feathers
covered the dead elk as the chain of life continued. The
air was filled with the sound of buzzing blowflies and
squawking birds.

They had spent the last months living on buffalo
tongue and meat. When they left, they swore they
would never eat a buff steak again. When they had first
ridden up the mountain, the wild game seemed plenti-

ful, and there were signs and tracks everywhere you went. That was not the case now. He was lucky to find this lone elk. Something told him the game was scarce this year, and they had finally got a stroke of luck. At least they wouldn't go hungry during the two weeks it took to get down the mountains.

They had timed it as closely as possible so they could kill as many buffalo as they could. They had taken two months to locate the herd; then the slaughter was quick. What took them the longest was skinning the animals and scraping the hides. All this had to be done on the spot. Now, they had seen enough of the Rocky Mountains and bison, and the brothers looked forward to spending some time in some semblance of civilization again. At least somewhere warm to wait out the winter. By summer, they would have their hides ready for sale. Maybe even in time for next year's Rendezvous.

When Ely pulled up to a stop, his brothers unloaded the mule and got to work on the steaks while he unsaddled his horse, brushed it down, and hobbled it with the rest. They cut a half dozen thick slabs of meat and put the rest on rock salt so it didn't spoil in the late summer heat. Elroy and Ernest did the honors, and the smell of grilled steak filled their senses in minutes.

The meat sizzled over the coals spitting fat, and freshly perked coffee mingled in the air. They might have smelled the sweat and bear fat if they weren't so focused on the food. Then again, these men were more professional buffalo killers than mountain men. Sure, they spent time in the mountains, but they didn't live there like Rusty Steel and Mountain Dennis. They were a breed apart from the rest. They came to slaughter the Indians' buffalo in as large of numbers as possible. They did it for the price of the hide and the tongue, which was considered a delicacy back East.

In a short time, all three men had chunks of elk meat stacked on their tin pie pans. As they ate, the only sound was chomping teeth as they tore at the tasty treat. It was miles apart from the tough buffalo they had eaten in the last months. Elk meat was considered of the highest quality available in the Rockies.

"I reckon we've got all the food we need for the rest of the trip," Ely said. "There's plenty of water along the trail, and there'll be steaks for every supper, and we've always got our stock of black beans. I reckon we're in pretty good shape."

"I long for a sip of corn liquor," Elroy said. He could almost taste the whiskey just by thinking about it. "I ain't been drunk for over three months."

"But now, do ya see why I said no liquor?" Ely asked. "We had a problem-free season huntin', and we ain't lost our scalps. There will be plenty of time to drink once we get out of the mountains. Gettin' drunk in the wilderness with Indians all around ain't the smartest thing to do. Everything has its time and place."

"I don't know that I can hold out for two more weeks," Elroy said gloomily. The way he talked, it sounded like he missed an old friend.

"Getting you sober for three months was probably the best thing for ya, brother," Ely said. "Your hands have stopped shakin', and you carry your load when ya ain't drunk on your butt."

"He's just a boy growin' into a man," Earnest said with care. You could see his feeling for his younger brother in his eyes. He protected him like a mother. "I remember back when you were a boy, and you weren't much different."

Ely tapped his temple with his finger and said, "The difference is here, brother."

Elroy was the only brother with a drinking problem. Sure, they all drank, but Elroy never knew when to quit; the more he drank, the more he wanted. Ely made a mental note to stay clear of his brother for the first few days once they arrived back in civilization. He hated it when he was sloshed and obnoxious. He would let him go off on one of his benders, then pick him up at the sheriff's office a few days later, as usual. The worst kind of drunk was the one with no idea of when to stop.

Nobody knew why the youngest, Elroy, turned to drink. The older brothers felt they had to take care of him, so he didn't get shot, but in general, he was a pleasant drunk and mostly played the clown for a few laughs and maybe a free shot of whiskey. However, he habitually went too far, angering the wrong people in the process. So, often Ely and Earnest would have to rush to get him out of trouble. Often as not, he would end up in jail for a night or three to sleep it off.

Of course, the three men carried a brace of pistols, each beside their buffalo guns. No White men traveled these woods and mountains without extra protection. Usually, one shot wouldn't do the trick, but with three or four, you at least had more of a chance. So far, they had only run into one group of Indian hunters interested in the same herd of buffalo. Ely had sent them packing with a couple of shots from nearly a mile away.

He didn't shoot at them, but he did place his bullets close enough to scare the dickens out of the braves. The natives immediately realized there was no way for them to get close enough to the buffalo hunters to kill them and not get killed in the process, so they'd begrudgingly left the herd to look for another.

The Crow warriors made a mental note and hoped they ran into these same White men somewhere down the trail. Maybe they would even hunt them after they were done with the buffalo. How dare they run off the landowners so they could butcher much more than they needed to eat? Eventually, the buffalo hunters became the enemy of all the Plains Indians. Had they known what was coming, they would have fought more arduously. It was too late, as the hordes of American Europeans were already on their way.

# RUSTY STEEL

LEVI AND RUSTY WERE SITTING AT THE PORCH TABLE playing another round of backgammon. Lately, every afternoon they challenged each other's skills at the ancient Asian game. In the wilderness, chess, dominos, checkers, and backgammon were common ways to pass the time and challenge the mind simultaneously. Of course, everybody played cards too. One of Levi's favorites was pitch.

"That's four out of five." Levi Johnson grinned like a possum. "I beat cha again."

"Dagnabit, I can count," Rusty Steel grumbled. "Double or nothin'. I've never lost so many games, not to mention to a young whippersnapper like you."

"I don't know if I dare play ya for four bits." Levi laughed. "I'd hate to take your money again. At this rate, I should have your last winter's earnings by summer."

"You just wait until you play Dennis," Rusty growled. "There must be one of us here that can beat cha. Angus will be back from the Crow camp soon. His wife only tolerates him for a couple of weeks at a time.

He be wicked clever when it comes to board games. I reckon he be both the laziest of the bunch and the smartest—at least until you and Forrester showed up. The one-armed captain has impressed me at every turn. He's already trying to ignore his handicap by making the rest of his body stronger. I saw him shoot his rifle the other day, and he didn't do too bad considerin' how heavy it is. I figure he'll have it down pat in a month or two."

"When is Angus comin' back?" Levi asked. "He's also the funniest of the lot."

"Whatcha mean by that?" Rusty retorted as he took offense. "I'm just as funny as any man in our compound."

"You're funny, all right." Levi smiled as his eyes twinkled. "Funny for you. Maybe you don't notice, but you are often the only one laughing at your jokes."

"Well, maybe I have better taste than you boys." Rusty laughed. "You can say whatever ya want, but I know who's the funniest of the bunch, and that be me. Heck, I'm an all-around wonder of modern science, I am. I'm intelligent, funny, a first-class mountain man, and even a better taleteller than most. Until you came to our little compound, I was the best shot, too. I figure by now, we must be pretty much a tie. You're reloading much faster than before. There ain't nothing like having a hostile Indian on your tail to learn to reload as fast as you can."

"So, what about Angus and his wife?" Levi asked again. "Will she be comin' with 'em?"

"That all depends on how long Green Leaf can tolerate the old fool." Rusty chuckled. "She likes to show him off at the tribe's powwows with his fancy dancing. The Indians all like to dance and pound drums. I reckon that's why so many Indian women fancy old Angus. I can't remember when he didn't have some girlfriend or wife somewhere. I know a couple died on 'em. Both were givin' birth. I figure the good Lord ain't got intentions for Angus to have children. He probably figures with one like him, we've got plenty."

Levi wrinkled up his nose and sniffed the air like an old hound dog. "I smell burnin' wood."

"A forest fire?" Rusty asked. He knew his sense of smell didn't match Dennis's or Levi's. The blood drained from his face. All of God's creatures were terrified of forest fires.

Levy stepped off the porch and looked behind the cabin. There, in the sky, was a trail of black smoke. Somebody had built a sizable fire, and some of the wood appeared green. It left a dark, ugly trail across cloudless heavens.

"It looks more like a campfire to me," Levi said as he searched the sky for signs of vultures. "I doubt it be settlers, but it is summertime, and some fools get so lost they have no idea where they are. I've run into folks like that all the way from Kansas City. Whoever it is, we've got company. Then again, they might pass right by without noticing the cabins."

"I don't like leavin' the livestock alone," Rusty said. "The other boys are out huntin' for nuts, berries, and fish for our food stock. Winters get long, and some salted trout comes in handy to challenge the taste buds. At least there's no lack of life in the rivers. The only problem with that is the grizzlies are also eating the salmon this time of year. It's a major part of their diet, but this ain't our boys' first rodeo. They'll be fine."

Levi continued to stare at the smoke as it snaked out of the trees and into the sky. He wondered how far it could be seen and who else might see it. Sure, they made a fire before the porch of an evening, but everybody on the mountain knew they were there, and they kept their fires to a minimum. The less presence you presented, the better odds you had of not being discovered by the wrong people.

"I can go down and sneak up on 'em to see who they are and what they be up to," Levi said. "They'll never know I was there. I can sneak up on a rattlesnake without leaving a track." Levi grinned as he baited his new friend.

"You sure are full of yourself, no doubt about that." Rusty laughed. "Then again, I reckon you've done proved yourself to the boys and me. Go on then, but don't make contact even iffin you think they be friendly. They might look innocent enough, but out here in the wilderness, half the men ya run into are outlaws or just mean and ornery—not to mention the Indians. Go on, get your horse saddled. Don't make me wait all day, either. It'll be safer if ya come back before nightfall. Both for you and me. I don't see Dennis and the boys riding in this late, but then again, you never know."

Levi headed for the stables. The remaining horses raced around the corral when he neared. Small clouds of dust chased their hooves. They were all feeling their oats and ready to get some exercise. From the few left, Johnson split off his horse, Tack, and saddled him up. He straddled his gray and squeezed its flanks with his calves, and they trotted toward the smoke. He figured it wasn't over a mile or two away, but then again, distances were difficult to judge in the mountains. What looked like it was ten minutes away could take a half day to get there and vice versa. The lack of a breeze made the smoke sit in the air as it slithered higher.

*If they're outlaws, they're too close for comfort,* Levi thought.

Then again, they could be lost settlers, like Rusty said. He knew from his travels from Indiana that thieves were found everywhere you went, and you usually didn't realize it until it was too late. If experience told him anything, it told him to tread lightly and cautiously. It would be easy enough to walk into a trap or stumble into the wrong camp.

Levi made his way toward the smoke, ensuring he was downwind just in case there were Indians around. About halfway there, he dropped off his horse and led him by the reins. The dead leaves absorbed most of the sound of Tack's hooves, and Levi didn't make a sound as he traveled. He stopped, closed his eyes, and took a deep breath. He smelled various odors.

Overpowering everything else was the smell of cooking meat and coffee. He tied Tack behind a stand of trees well out of sight and continued on foot. As he walked, the smells got stronger. He crouched for a moment as he reassessed the situation, but now the smell of sweat came from two distinct directions. This gave Levi pause, and he lay on his belly and moved forward a foot at a time. He strained, listening for any out-of-place sounds. It wouldn't be the first time a hunter found himself the one being hunted, and Levi didn't plan to fall into that trap.

Above all, he had to remain unseen. He finally got close enough and parted the brush with his fingers. That was when he saw the three hunters feasting on fresh elk steaks. The smell of meat made his mouth water. The problem was he also noted the distinct smell of bear fat, which he knew only Indians used. But he couldn't see the hostiles. They, like him, were masters at hiding and sneaking up on people. It was apparent that whoever else was watching, they weren't friendlies. They had to be hostiles, but from what tribe?

Levi inched forward as close as he dared and ensured he still wasn't seen. Not just by the buffalo hunters but also by whoever was watching them. Now, things had suddenly gotten much more complicated. Hopefully, they hadn't noticed him, or he might lead them back home, and he and Rusty would be hard-bent on taking on a war party. Most Indians didn't travel outside of their tribes alone. It was far too dangerous, especially from their sworn enemies, which was every other tribe that lived in the mountains and the plains. Few were friends and nearly all were foes.

Levi watched as the buffalo hunters feasted on a freshly killed elk. They had been lucky but maybe not as fortunate as they thought. He knew somebody else was waiting out there spying on the White men. He was torn between helping the hunters because they came from his race or leaving them to their fate for killing harmless animals in the hundreds for money. Eventually, this mass slaughter left the Indians with less than half the food of only two years prior. He wanted to wait until he saw everybody he would have to deal with if things went south as they often did in the Rockies.

It was getting late as the disk of fire neared the horizon. In an hour, the night would come. Johnson wondered if the Indians planned to attack at dusk or at dawn. He was sure they weren't waiting out there for the fun of it. They were after blood or horses, or maybe both. That was when he heard a horse neigh and another answer. He saw them grazing on the other side of the clearing. They were all hobbled for the night.

He remembered back to what the Sioux war chief, Chaska, had said. They had expected thirty-three warriors, and only twenty-six arrived. The war chief had said something about his men losing their horses, which was why they came on foot. It was the same horses he ran off in the middle of the night. In the end, had they ridden into the attack, the outcome would have been dramatically different for the Indians. Above the dynamite were sacks of nails, so they would spray any rider that rode past when the explosion went off. Anything below six feet was safe from flying metal objects. Everything above would be cut to pieces, horses included.

Levi turned his mind back to the present. Could these be the same missing horses? He counted over thirty, but Levi wasn't good at counting livestock like ranchers were. He had been around animals but never herds of horses or cattle. Now, he focused on the object of the most interest—the waiting braves. Could they be the missing Sioux Indians? He started to put the pieces of the puzzle together. That was when he saw the bushes rustle slightly on the opposite side of the camp. Levi buried his face in the dirt.

He waited, hoping not to be discovered. After some time, he silently pulled grass from his surroundings and stuck it in his hair. Now he looked like part of the brush. His face was covered in the dirt in which he lay. He was more difficult to see. He risked another peek. His heart skipped a beat as he glanced around to see if he had been seen.

That was when he caught a glimpse of a Crow warrior down near the horses. Could two Indian war parties be targeting the same animals, and Levi was out there alone with them? He knew if he tried to back out now, he risked being seen. So he stared through the hole he'd made in the bushes and waited as the glowing sun slowly closed its eye on the horizon. Rays of light flashed out in a kaleidoscope of color, thrusting skyward like pointed teeth.

Crickets started to chirp, and lightning bugs flashed off and on in the distance. Levi patiently sat to see what would happen next. His Hawken rifle lay beside his shoulder, but he didn't want to start any trouble. At this point, his only objective was to extract himself from the area. With the possibility of two war parties from different tribes and three buffalo hunters, he knew nothing but bad could come from the collision of destinies. It appeared that the only one who knew where all the parties were was him, although none of them knew Levi was hidden, watching as his head pounded between his ears. His mouth was so dry his lips stuck to his teeth.

Of course, everybody within sight of the smoke had to know where the White men were. They had notified every Indian within miles with their big fire—tinting the sky black. Now, it was time to see who moved first. Levi watched and listened intently. He knew when it came, his window of time would be small, if not very small. He would have to be ready and move as quickly and silently as possible.

He had to get back to the cabin and warn Rusty. At

least there, they could make a stand. As it was, Levi would be a sitting duck for the first group that spotted him. He was outnumbered on all sides, and everybody was out to draw blood. He saw no way out of this one. If only some distraction came. As he stared, he silently prayed to God to give him one more chance, and he promised to read the Bible daily.

That was when he realized he needed a miracle to get out of what he had gotten himself into. If he made it out, he promised to be less arrogant and think things through rather than trying to show off what a good mountain man he was. He figured that must be part of the lesson: to be humble about what you do and don't know. Levi sighed, almost like the thought gave him relief. He blinked his eyes and emptied his lungs as a weight was lifted from his shoulders.

# MOUNTAIN DENNIS

RUSTY STEEL PACED BACK AND FORTH ON HIS CABIN'S porch. The wood planks groaned under his feet. He wore a frown with a furrowed brow as he narrowed his eyes. Every few minutes, he would look off into the distance to see if the smoke was still there. He had his rifle in his fists and three pistols stuffed in a wide belt. As soon as Levi had left, he'd gotten a bad feeling. He had taken a liking to the young mountain man. He saw a reflection of his young self in young Levi Johnson.

It was just like when his old captain had helped him all those years ago on the docks of St. Louis. He quickly took a boy and turned him into a man. He wanted to help Levi avoid many of the same mistakes he had made, but that wasn't working out well.

He fingered the bear claws on his necklace as his mind raced for all the different things that could happen. The teeth on his bracelet had yellowed with time. Much of the Rocky Mountains was still cloaked in mystery; if you lived there before long, you found the unexpected was always around the corner. It could be any one of a million things.

He wondered if the boys would return from the hunt before nightfall or would arrive tomorrow. He knew they wouldn't linger on their laurels if Mountain Dennis was in charge. Bill Forrester was still a soldier, took pride in everything he did, and complied with every order to the smallest detail. He had never seen a man so meticulous. Rusty knew he shouldn't leave the compound alone, especially with strangers on the mountain. Who else might be out there with them?

On their first hunt, Levi and he had done the honors, but the wild game was scarce, and they spent days scaring up a couple of elk along with the deer. There was no sign at all of the buffalo. Rusty knew how sometimes the moon affected the wild animals. With a full moon, they were nervous and quick to flee, sprinting for cover. This made it harder to sneak up on them. Then again, Rusty Steel had a lot of theories, some from some things he was told and other things he read.

On nights when they had a newspaper, he would read to the men by the yellow light of the porch lantern. They were all ears on these occasions. A couple of the boys couldn't correctly read and write. It was also a form of entertainment. Over the week, he would read the newspaper word for word, and of course, the night was full of Rusty's personal comments. It came in the package, and he had opinions on everything—some sound, and others not so much so.

He also had to be careful that he didn't drop Levi into the muck by chasing after him like he was a child. After thinking on the subject, he deducted he would just draw more attention to his friend even if he could locate where he was, which was doubtful. It was his first instinct and strongest urge, but he had proven he was a long sight from a child. Still, the question ate at him: was he going to be all right and make it back before dark like Rusty told him, or was he going to run into problems like most ventures out of the compound?

The boys were riding with Sam, Bob, and Pete, so if they showed up in time, they would have reinforcements to fend off an attack. But alone or even with Levi, it would still be a stretch. Angus was in his wife's Crow camp, oblivious to what was happening back at the cabins.

"He ain't even my kin but just the same, I feel responsible for him like he was a nephew," Rusty said to himself out loud. "I wonder if he'll make it back without gettin' winged. I know I shouldn't have let 'em go, but who am I to tell a grown man what to do?"

At this point, Levi Johnson knew almost as much as Rusty about survival in this dangerous environment. He'd already proved he could out-track them and had displayed he was a sharpshooter too. Until then, they hadn't found a thing in the wilderness in which he didn't excel. He'd even made his own original traps that worked better than the store-bought product. Only his reluctance to shoot ornery men puzzled the others. Maybe once he lived a few more years up there, he'd realize some men were meant to be shot and killed. Some men and a few women that walked the earth were as wicked and evil as the devil himself.

In the last minutes of the day, Rusty saw the silhouettes of five men riding in his direction. They were coming down the same trail Dennis and the boys left on. He pulled out his spyglass, and the objects jumped out at him like they were only feet away. Dennis led at a trot with Forrester's white stallion prancing beside him. The white horse dwarfed the beige horse. After them came Sam, Pete, and Bob. They had the string line with the mules in tow. They were loaded down with meat and even eight buffalo furs. They would have plenty to eat for the winter.

"How'd it go?" Rusty asked as they neared the porch on horseback. "You boys look knackered and the horses worn out. I'll go make up a pot of coffee. It'll take the chill off from sittin' out here on the porch at night and wake you boys up so you can make it through your meal."

"We didn't find but a few elk, but we did find a small herd of buffalo. There were plenty, but we only took eight buffs in all," Dennis said. "That gives us enough salted meat for the winter and a buffalo skin robe each. There must have been ten thousand bison in all but nothing like a couple of years ago. Either that or they're grazing somewhere else."

"They ain't grazing somewhere else," Bob huffed. "There's a thousand White hunters out there killin' 'em off faster than they can reproduce. We only took what we needed, but they be fine specimens." He smiled as the setting sun flashed off his front gold teeth.

Sam, Pete, and Bill were still covered in dried blood. They had obviously been gutting and cleaning bison, and the stench followed them.

"Before you come into my house, I expect you to clean all that blood and guts off your hands and faces," Rusty said as he eyed Forrester before glancing at the others. "No offense, and I'm sure you did your part just fine, but you stink to beat the dickens. All you boys go and clean up, and I'll scare up somethin' to eat. We'll store the salted meat in the cellar."

Dennis returned first and wore clean clothes, but his fingernails were still dirty. They were caked with blood. None of them smelled like butchers any longer, so Rusty welcomed them in to eat. He'd made black beans with smoked pork and strips of bacon to slap between hot biscuits. All six men were famished, and nobody talked until every scrap was gone.

Dennis looked around and asked, "Where's your boy Levi? I thought you two stuck together like pine tree sap."

"Have a look down there," Rusty said. Concern etched across his face. "Quick now, the sun's givin' out."

Dennis grinned and asked, "What is it?" He went up, walked across the porch, and looked in the direction Rusty nodded. He frowned as soon as he saw a thin black stream of smoke from a campfire. It ran up and out of sight from the treetops—there wasn't a breath of air.

"Why, that's gotta be visible for miles," Dennis said. "How far away do you figure that be?"

"It's hard to say because the air is so still. It could be a couple of miles or maybe even five," Rusty said. "That's where Levi went. He was supposed to come back here before dark. It don't look like he's gonna make it."

"What? You didn't send him out there alone, did ya?" Dennis asked, taken aback. "That was a foolish thing to do."

"He's a grown man and a woodsman. Plus, I didn't send him anywhere," Rusty retorted. "I didn't like the idea any more than you do, but I can't tell a grown man what to do any more than I can tell you what not to do. I didn't want him to go, but you know how young folks be. They have a mind of their own. It looks like you did well on the hunt. After the first bad run, I figured you wouldn't find much of anything. In the end, y'all got lucky. At least business has been good this year."

"Don't change the subject. You know as well as I do when we see somebody come a visitin' unannounced, we always arm up, close the other two cabins, and batten down the hatches here," Dennis said just as Forrester stepped from the cabin to the porch. "Your cabin has the best field of fire."

"Field of fire?" ex-Captain Forester asked. "What's going on now, boys?"

Rusty didn't answer but instead pointed to the sky in the distance.

Bill smiled and said, "We've got company. I believe having someone new to talk to is good, isn't it?"

"Uninvited company up here ain't ever good," Rusty grumbled. "Levi's gone out there to see if he can get close and have a look at who they be and what they're up to."

"That is just like, Levi," Forrester said. "Running off before I got back in time to go with him. Now he's going to have all the fun himself."

Rusty and Dennis completely ignored such nonsense. They didn't answer, which puzzled Bill. There was no way they would let Forrester go out into the dark looking for a camp. It could be full of hostiles —red or white.

"What time did ya first see the smoke?" Dennis asked.

"I reckon it was in the afternoon," Rusty replied.

"Plenty long enough for every Indian in the mountains to have seen it. You do know half of them will go and have a peek. There are no cures for curiosity or stupidity. I'd swear they're related."

"Well, why ain't we goin' after him if it's not good news?" Forrester asked.

"You just let us think about planning this one," Rusty said. "This is probably about Indians, and West Point don't know squat about the tribes except what they read in the newspapers. The rest of that stuff in your head is just clutter, so let it go and watch and learn."

Rusty sat, pushed his chair against the wall, and blew out a long exhale of smoke as he thought about what to do next. He knew he had taken it just about as far as he could. Sometimes, things had a mind of their own and happened no matter how well you thought or planned. He knew to run after Levi in the dark would be twice as dangerous. Then they would have the added danger of having Levi sneaking around the forest armed to the teeth. None of them wanted to get shot, especially not by a friend.

They were going to have to wait unless something direr happened. At the moment, only one group member hadn't shown up after a walkabout. A hundred different things could have occurred, but they would have to wait to hear the story from Levi. At least they would if he returned. When that time would come, he couldn't be exactly sure.

"I don't like it any more than you fellas do, but we're gonna have to wait here until morning to do anything," Rusty said. "Going out at night with who knows how many Indians out there ain't a good idea. Then there are the fools that lit such a big fire and have been stoking it all day long. They've gotta be White men. Who else would do such a fool thing in Indian Territory?"

Seven of the compound's occupants sat on the porch waiting for some sign of Levi Johnson. Rusty dozed off and on in his chair, tilted against the front of the cabin. He had given up trying to figure out a plan because he lacked information. They didn't know who they were facing or how many. Suppose they were Indians or White men or maybe both? The only answer to the current dilemma was patience.

They would just have to sit it out. The other boys played poker in the circle of yellow light cast by the lantern. Bill Forrester sat on the edge, dangling his feet as he wondered what was holding Levi up. It wasn't like him not to come back when he said, but he knew there wasn't a darned thing he could do right now.

Forrester was edgy and couldn't sit still, so he spent the night making coffee for the men. A jug of corn liquor sat beside the lamp. The orange tips of cheroots and pipe bowls glowed in the night, lighting up the faces of the smokers. They all seemed deep in thought and hardly spoke the whole night.

A rooster crowed from the chicken house.

# WORLDS COLLIDE

COYOTES CALLED OUT IN THE DARK OF NIGHT, BUT LEVI was sure they were men, not animals. He had heard the Comanche replicate the sound exactly, and his gut told him no coyotes would come so close to so many people. They were afraid of humans, especially the White men with the big fire. Then he heard owls from the other side of the campsite. They could be genuine, or they could be the Indians from what he suspected was another tribe.

Levi didn't know if they saw the smoke or were tracking the hunters to steal their horses or to right some wrong. At the moment, the only thing that wasn't a mystery was the reckless mountain men around the fire. The piles of buffalo hides disclosed their trade— that and their long rifles. He knew how much Rusty emphasized that they only take the buffalo they needed for food and robes.

Steel claimed the buffalo were special for all the Plains Indians and always had been. When they think someone infringes on their buffalo, their disposition could change in a minute. The hate ran deep for those men who killed them by the hundreds and thousands. Just because of who they were, Levi knew they would instantly be the Indians' enemy, and it didn't matter the tribe.

The hunters gathered enough wood to last all night. This wasn't some typical campfire but a roaring blaze in a clearing of trees. The fire was visible only if you got close, but the smoke snaked into the sky all day. Cinders were visible in the night as they swirled around, shooting skyward on thermal currents. The fire's snap, pop, and crackle were heard above the White men's mumbles. At least they knew not to shout. They must have thought they were alone in the wilderness, when truth be known, it was rare that someone wasn't spying on travelers from afar.

Still, the buffalo hunters sat and continued to feast on the elk, oblivious to the surrounding danger. When they were done eating, they played dice. They gambled until the wee hours of the night. Levi could feel their eyes on the hunters. He wondered again if he would have time to escape. Maybe he should just cut and run. If it were only White men, he wouldn't think twice. But with Indians out there in the dark, the odds of making it to safety dropped dramatically. He looked to the east but still no signs of the first glimpse of daylight. The moon cast long silver shadows across the landscape.

Levi lay there trapped. At least the Indians hadn't attacked at dusk. With any luck, they would wait until dawn. By then, he hoped to escape from his hiding place. The only time they left the camp was to go to the edge of the circle of light provided by the fire to take a leak. The flames made shadows dance on the trees. An evening breeze blew up and made the tops sway.

Johnson stared hard at the east and blinked his eyes. He rubbed them with the heels of his hands and looked toward the first vestiges of light. He pulled the brush aside and looked again. Two mountain men were sound asleep with their horses hobbled nearby. A third sat away from the fire with a rifle on his lap. Pistol grips stuck out of his pants. He was clever enough to sit in the shadows and not by the campfire. It wasn't easy to see him until the sun rose. Levi could just make out his outline. He wondered who he was.

He sucked in a few deep breaths, steadying himself for what was to come. He tried to calm down and figure out which way he was going to run. His heart stopped for a second. Everything seemed to freeze. When it passed, the quiet ended, and his heart redlined. A cacophony of bullets and arrows flew through the air. He could see the Crow Indians and the buffalo hunters return fire with deadly precision.

Levi Johnson was hidden at the flank of the battle. The hunters reacted much faster than expected. They returned fire with three Hawken buffalo guns and an array of pistols. Bullets slammed into trees and Indians alike. A heavy caliber round went through one Indian and into a second, only to ricochet off a rock behind two dead men. Their firepower was an awesome thing.

The Sioux Indians wanted the horses back that the buffalo hunters had stolen so they could finally go home. The hunters knew they had come for the live-stock. Seven warriors fought against heavy caliber rifles, but it was a losing battle with only bows and arrows. There were too many trees to hide behind. The White men were so skillful they could shoot the legs off a tadpole.

The Sioux Indians followed the buffalo hunters with the horses. They had them in their sights, and their animals were right behind them. They would have to go through the White men to get to the small herd. If they failed, they would never be allowed to return home. There was no choice: they had to capture the horses.

The Crow Indians whom the buffalo hunters had run off the killing fields had followed the White men to their camp. They weren't interested in old nags and horses with burned-out lungs. Later, they had seen all the red carcasses rotting in the sun. They'd seen how their enemies wasted their buffalo, so they came for revenge. The hunters were pinned down between the Sioux and the Crow. Suddenly, they noticed arrows fall from the other side. The sun had yet to rise, making everything look hazy. It was that in-between moment when night transitioned into the day.

Levi could see Crow Indians to his right. They were attacking the hunters. On the left stood Sioux warriors. They appeared to be waiting to see how things panned out, although some halfheartedly flung arrows. What they wanted was their horses back. That was where their eyes were focused.

The Crow intended to take the lives of the White men. If the Crow did the dangerous work for the Sioux, all the better. Then they could deal with the Crow after they had suffered casualties and were low on ammunition, whether powder or arrows. They could only fight for a certain period before they had nothing to throw at them, and they knew they would never be able to sneak up on them, even in the dark. If they did, more would die.

The White men hid behind rocks and stumps of dead trees, but now they had fire to their rear. They could only move to their flanks or try to break through the lines and defeat the enemy. Levi counted seven Crow Indians and five Sioux, who looked more like hunters than warriors. At least they didn't have scalps sewn into their buckskins like warriors he had seen— that or hanging on their belts. If you took a scalp, it was worthless unless you showed it off. Then your peers could see how dangerous you were.

Levi saw what was going to happen. The White hunters would run for one of their flanks as soon as the Sioux showed themselves and joined in on the attack. After that, they would undoubtedly fight each other for the price of hides and horses. Levi wanted to ensure he wasn't there when they came his way. Luck hadn't been on his side lately, and he didn't think now was a good time to tempt things.

While the three enemies battled each other, Levi backed out of there like a rat out of a hole. He turned, then snaked his way out on his belly, making sure not to rustle the bushes. When he was deep in the trees, he stopped and turned back to the violence. Now, he could see the two Indian tribes exchanging fire and arrows. Everybody was hunkered down, with the buffalo hunters in the middle. They had been stupid, and rather than escaping for one of their flanks, they tried to hide and shoot from cover. It was plausible when they faced one group of hostile warriors, but with two, it left them pinned down. Their window of time had escaped them, and now they were the ones trapped.

The sun broke over the horizon, shooting yellow rays of light across the sky. The stars slowly rolled back like a carpet until they all disappeared. Shadowy figures of men fighting suddenly became crystal clear. More Indians began to drop as the Sioux moved into battle mode. Now there was no turning back.

When Levi had crawled on his belly far enough away, he jumped to his feet and ran for his life. If he were lucky, the Crow hunters, the Sioux warriors, and three White men would kill each other off. Suddenly, he stopped. He knew he should flee, but something kept him frozen on the spot. He was deep enough into the woods that he didn't have to worry about arrows, but a bullet might get by. Still, he just stood there and stared like he was having an out-of-body experience. He witnessed the battle from afar, completely detached mentally. It was like he was watching an old nightmare in slow motion. Nobody gained any ground during the first hour of fire.

Levi hid in the long shadows of first light. He closed his eyes and took a deep breath through his nose. The smell of cordite was strong in the air, mixed with the acrid smell of blood. As he stood there observing, he felt his heart race and realized the Indians had bitten off more than they could chew.

Even outnumbered more than three to one, the hunters, with their skilled marksmanship, deflected every attack. They shot them like they were floating ducks at the carnival. Still, the situation had turned into a stalemate. Now with the light, nobody could sneak away or sneak up on anybody. The buffalo hunters waited patiently for a target.

Levi could hardly hear himself think. His mind was

spinning so fast that he couldn't settle down enough to decide calmly what to do. He saw the horses. They were the same ones he'd run off from the Sioux war party. If they found him, they wouldn't be friendly. Then again, they had their hands full right now.

Suddenly, he heard horses' hooves pounding the earth and coming closer. A haze of dust churned behind the riders. A man on a sturdy mustang and another man with yellow hair on a white stallion led the party. Five more White men with rifles came in at a gallop. They were riding like their hair was on fire. Levi knew he had to warn them before they rode into the middle of a battle. He jumped to his feet, waving his arms like mad. Rusty's sharp eye instantly saw him and turned their horses for the young man from Indiana.

As soon as the men from the cabins showed up, the Indians cowered. The Crow seemed confused now; so many people had assembled in one place, and almost all were enemies.

"Whew, that was a close one," Levi said, visibly shaken.

He walked out of the forest not fifty feet from the hunters. He surprised them with his appearance. The six men on horseback clearly meant all business. Johnson grinned like a possum.

Forrester raced up with a pistol in his fist and his reins in his teeth. He had changed, and now he appeared even more dangerous. He pulled up to such a hard stop his horse almost sat down.

Bill jumped off and huffed, "Are ya all right, partner? You had us worried there for a moment. It looks like you had things under control."

"Didn't you see the Crow and the Sioux?" Levi

asked. "I came an inch from losing my scalp. I saw no control here until y'all arrived. I reckon the trouble be with those three. They've war parties riled up on both sides. Lucky for them, they were crack shots, or this would end differently."

Everybody stopped firing when the six armed mountain men came racing to the scene. Three battling elements had just encountered a new danger, even stronger and more perilous. The Crow Indians instantly recognized Rusty Steel and Mountain Dennis. White Weasel caught their eyes and nodded. The mountain man gave him a scolding grumble.

Steel stood in his stirrups and shouted in English, "Hold on a dadgum minute! That means you, boys," he said in Crow. He used his limited Sioux to say stop and parley. It wasn't a request. It was an order. "Did you say Crow and Sioux both?" Rusty asked Levi, confused. "I wonder what got under the Sioux skin. What I would like to know is how all of us happened to be in the same place in the middle of the wilderness."

The Indians stopped and listened to the voice of reason. They hadn't intended to find themselves in such a position. It was one thing taking revenge or stealing White men's horses, but it would be an overwhelming battle if the other seven joined in. They all saw Levi emerge from the trees not fifteen yards from the edge of the campsite. Everybody seemed puzzled, but one and all looked at Rusty. There was a quality in his voice that said, Listen to what I have to say or else.

"Whatcha doin' trying to kill White men on our mountain?" Rusty asked in Crow. "We've let each other be for as long as I can remember. Why do ya wanna start trouble now?"

"We finally found a herd of bison, and they shot their guns at us, chasing us off our land and forbidding us to hunt for food. We came here to take back the furs —our furs. We didn't know the Sioux were there too, or we would have held back."

"What have you three fools got to say for yourselves?" Rusty spat as he gave the buffalo hunters a hard stare. "It's morons like you three that make it impossible to live in peace up here. Why don't you go shoot buffalo somewhere else? This is our mountain, and it's crawlin' with hostile Indians. You be fools to hunt here anyway."

"Who do you think you are to tell us what to do?" Ely Grimms snarled. "My brothers and me don't bow down to nobody. Especially Injun lovers."

You could see the hunter steel up before Rusty. As he walked their way, Rusty got down. But not before Levi reached him. Beaver moved in so quickly that they couldn't stop him. All the gun barrels were pointed toward the ground. He landed a decisive blow to Ely's solar plexus. The air whooshed out of his lungs, and down he went as he gasped and struggled to breathe. Levi grabbed him by the belt and pulled him up enough to arch his back to make breathing easier. Rusty still wanted answers, and unconscious men don't talk.

The buffalo hunter blew out a snort instantly, followed by a cynical glare. He had a smirk on his face as he said, "I'm an American, and it's a free country, ain't it? That means my brothers and me can go wherever we want to go. Ain't you or anybody else is gonna stop us, either." He didn't see any negotiating in Rusty's hard, fierce eyes. It was about to escalate in the next few seconds.

"I have met some stupid people in my time, but you

three take the cake," Rusty said. "Levi, leave 'em be, but don't you dare get up until you hear what I've gotta say. First, tell me, where did ya get the horses?"

"We found 'em wandering in the forest," Ernest said. "We looked all around for the owners, but they didn't show up. We ain't horse thieves, mister. We only took 'em because they were abandoned."

"Hey, Rusty," Levi said. "Them's the same horses I ran off with the Sioux war party. That must be the men War Chief Chaska sent to find 'em. I've got bad news for you three gentlemen. Those horses belong to the Crow Indians."

"And which one is Crow?" Elroy asked. "I figure one Injun is the same as another."

"Your Sioux is better than mine, Dennis," Rusty said. "Tell 'em to get their horses and skedaddle out of here. Tell 'em I know their boss, Chaska. We won't give 'em no trouble iffin they don't give us any."

"You ain't givin' our horses away, fool," Ely spat.

The backhand came so fast he didn't see but a blur right before Levi's massive paw slapped him upside the head. It knocked him to the ground yet again. This time his head spun, and he saw stars. Ely pushed himself up in the sitting position and shook his head. He looked at Levy and then over to Rusty.

"What else do you want us to do?" Ely said, but you could hear the malice.

Rusty shot him an indifferent smirk. "Are you two gonna give me problems like your brother here? If you are, let's get to it. You two, and Levi and me. Come on now. Have ya suddenly got shy? Just a minute ago, you were talking all brave and full of yourselves."

On the other side of the camp, the four survivors of

the Sioux war party rounded up their horses and mounted up to drive them home. Dark Horse lay across a horse's back. He had a hole the size of an orange in his back.

He had been the first man to die. He would never see his wife and infant son again. At least some of the Crow warriors would get to return home to their families.

"I'm afraid you're gonna have to forfeit all your buffalo hides," Rusty said. "It's one thing shooting at a herd you found yourself, but it is an entirely different matter when you shoot at the Indians who own the land the danged buffalo are on."

"And who do you think you are to tell us what to do?" Earnest asked. He didn't hide his disdain.

"I'm gonna let ya in on a secret, fools," Rusty said. "We be the meanest, oneriest, most dangerous White men in the Rocky Mountains. We're Indian fighters, hunt grizzlies for fun, and have races with mountain lions. Now, you tell me who's in charge here. You wannabes or us—real mountain men?"

"Why, Levi here could kick all your butts on his own; he only slapped you there, cuz." Dennis snickered. "He'll knock your block off if you get hit by his haymaker."

# TROUBLE

"LOOKEE OVER THERE," ELROY SAID AS HE STARED. HE was sure his voice was shaking. He was doing his best to hide it, but it was hard. He touched his side. "The last of the Injuns are leavin'. I reckon it's safe now. Things were lookin' pretty bad for a minute there."

Elroy's face was pale—shades of gray. This was the first time he had been face-to-face with such violence. He didn't want to repeat the experience.

"We had everything under control," Ely bragged. "I was who shot all of them Indians. One brother can't hit the side of a barn with a scattergun, and the other is too affable. If it weren't for me, you two would be nothin'."

"You got the biggest gift of all," Rusty said, all matter of fact like. "You got the gift of life. You were mighty near death, but you got to trade your furs and horses for your scalps. Don't you fellas think it's worth the trade? If not, just let me know, and I'll call them Sioux back to finish what they started."

"It's pure luck none of ya got shot by one of those arrows," Levi said as he looked at arrows everywhere, stuck into the ground or broken. "I'd say you got away by the skin of your teeth."

"What are y'all anyway?" Ely asked with a bad attitude. "Some kind of law? Nobody asked you to butt in. We were doin' just fine until you showed up. We were just mindin' our own business. You know as well as I do there ain't no law against huntin' buffalo—or Indians, for that matter. The army encourages men to go out and hunt in groups. We ain't the only men doin' what we're doin'."

"Yeah, but you're the only ones doing it where we live. If you wanna go rile up the Indians someplace else, be my guest," Rusty said. "But not on our mountain, you're not."

"What are we going to do with these men?" Bill Forrester asked. "They are right, you know. The army even provides protection to buffalo hunters at times."

"If it were up to me, I'd hang 'em by their feet and let the vultures peck their eyes out," Sam said as his eyes shot daggers at the hunters. "Your poor decisions and actions are what brought Indians to our mountain, and at the moment, we've already had a good dose. Iffin you keep messing with these warrior braves, you'll end up like me." He removed his hat and showed his scars. "You'll get scalped. I can guarantee you won't like it one bit when it happens to you. It's a miracle I survived. Most folks don't."

"The only law or army I see up here is you, Captain Forrester, and you ain't even army no more," Rusty snapped. "Up here, we make our own laws, and if you don't want to abide, you can scat right now and never come back!" He was yelling at the buffalo hunters again.

The Crow Indians had gathered up the hides,

loaded them on their horses, and led them into the woods on foot. They didn't have all that far to go. The Sioux vanished into the forest with their horses and their dead. It sure didn't seem like a few scraggly horses and a pile of buffalo hides was worth so much loss of life. Now, the mountain men were ready for the buffalo hunters to gather their things and get off their mountain. They were nothing but trouble. All the tribes hated the men who made a living killing their food supply. They knew that without the buffalo, they would cease to exist.

"Come on, you two," Ely spat as he turned to saddle up their horses. Their mules didn't carry a single buffalo hide. "There goes our whole summer earnings." He gave Levi and Rusty looks that would peel paint off a wall.

Elroy had been leaning against a tree. The blood drained from his face as his eyes rolled back in his head, and he fell to the ground, unconscious. When Ely felt his pulse, it was weak. His face glistened in sweat. His brother pulled up his shirt and gasped.

"Why, Elroy's been shot!" Ely cried. "Our little brother's in a bad way."

Forrester, who had studied basic first aid at the military academy, dismounted and kneeled beside the young hunter. He was clammy to the touch. He put his ear to his mouth and could hear the ragged breathing, short and fast.

"I'm afraid he's in shock," Forrester said. He inspected the entrance wound, which was as big as a walnut. "We've got to get him to the cabin so we can keep him warm and tend to his wound." He rolled him over, and the hole in his back was the size of an orange.

Forrester first locked eyes with Levi, then with Rusty. Finally, he looked at the two brothers and said, "We need to make up a travois quick and get him somewhere we can clean that wound and see if it hit any vitals. If it didn't, we can sew him up and wait and see what happens. I'm afraid it don't look too good for your younger brother."

Rusty didn't try to hide his displeasure. "I figure we should just let 'em fend for themselves. They didn't think much of the lives of the Indians or their food source. They didn't consider us livin' up here in the mountain with the Indians either. All they been doin' is thinking about themselves. It don't take all that much to set the local Indians off. You three fools brought two tribes nearly to our doorstep."

Levi's look of shock was so profound that Rusty was embarrassed by what he had said. He finally replied, "Ah, what the heck. Let's get that travois put together— the clock's tickin' boys. Maybe we can save this young man's life."

"How were we supposed to have known y'all lived around here?" Ely, the oldest brother, asked. "I don't see no signs that say No Trespassing. Who do you think you are, anyway?"

"If you press this, mister, your brother is gonna die," Levi whispered. They strained their ears to hear. "Rusty Steel don't take sass from nobody. Now, he offered you a place where we can try to save your brother's life. Whatcha wanna do? Stand here and argue and be a smart aleck, or do ya wanna try to help your brother?"

"Our brother," Earnest said. "He's more important, Ely. We've done enough harm here. Now we've got our little brother shot. If anything happens to him, Ma will skin us alive. I knew we should have picked someplace with less aggressive Indians."

"Hush up, fool," Ely spat. "Let's get a horse rigged up to take Elroy somewhere he can get treated. The less time we spend with this bunch, the better."

"One of us livin' up here has a Crow wife who tends to what ails us sometimes. I can't say for sure, but she may have a go at it. If not, Dennis and I will have to do unless you wanna try to patch 'em up," Rusty said.

"I've never had any experience with such injuries. My name's Ely, and this is my middle brother, Earnest. The winged one is Elroy, the youngest. We're the Grimms brothers. We've only been up here for three months or so. I hardly saw person one until the last few days, and it seems like we've run into every Indian on the mountain, not to mention you, fellas. Y'all be trappers, I take it. And how's that workin' out for ya?"

"If you're thinking about trappin' on our mountain, you've got another thing comin'," Sam spat. "Watch these fellas, boys. First, they come to kill off the buffalo, and next, they'll be trappin' out our streams."

Levi pulled a hatchet from his saddle and quickly cut down branches for Dennis, Rusty, and the brothers to make a travois. They put it together in thirty minutes. They carefully placed Elroy on it as they slowly led the horse with the wounded man. Blood pooled on the buffalo skin under Elroy's body. His breath was short and shallow. Levi hadn't seen that many wounded men, but the ones he had seen with such a wound rarely survived. The hole was just too big. Then again, one just never knew.

They had ridden down in minutes, but the climb

back up with the travois slowed them down and made the trip seem interminable. All the time, Levi was running out into the forest to look for more signs of Indians. Just because they had disappeared back where the battle had been and where the mountain men had gotten the drop on them didn't mean they wouldn't come back. What the mountain men considered a friendly conclusion the Sioux and Crow Indians might feel wasn't finished.

No White man knew what ran through the minds of the Indian warriors. There were a breed apart. They seemed to come from another world at a different time. They were fierce and had excellent skills, but at the same time, they were still primitive. Levi marveled at how they had evolved differently compared to the Europeans. Any race that had existed in solitude for ten thousand years would never understand the relatively modern American thinking, let alone the thoughts of the settlers.

"Of all the places you could have come to hunt buffalo, you had to come through our mountain. There must be a hundred different trails. This ain't the only one, ya know," Yosemite Bob said. "Nobody ever takes the time to think that people live up here. It may not look like it, but a few mountain men and even some wives have settled here to escape civilization. Nobody seems to consider that, for them, this is a simple case of trespassing and intrusion. None of them thought about those who had to spend their lives in these mountains. Y'all would never go to a house unannounced or hunt on somebody else's property without permission back East, would ya?"

Of the two brothers, Earnest seemed the most

worried. He walked beside the travois with a canteen and a bandana. Every few minutes, he wet the bandana and bathed his brother's face with cool water. Sweat dripped off his chin, and his shirt was stuck to his chest. The gaping wound was open. They didn't have anything to use to patch him up. He stuffed it with bandanas to stifle the flow of blood. His brother soaked the cloth and squeezed it above Elroy's mouth. Drops of water quenched his thirst. His mouth was so dry his tongue stuck to the roof of his mouth.

Ely didn't seem to notice Elroy's condition. It was like he was taking his existence for granted, and in the Rocky Mountains, nothing was a given. Still, he hardly glanced at Elroy, even though he looked like he was knocking on heaven's door. It wasn't long before they saw a wooden zigzag fence in the distance. Their horses whinnied, and the animals in the corral neighed.

"We're finally here, Elroy," Earnest said to his brother. He walked beside him holding his hand. His fear for his life was apparent. He was shaken by what had happened, while Ely acted like it was the bread and butter of every day.

In just over an hour, they arrived at the compound. The distance was short, but some trails were difficult to get by with the travois. Many of the paths from the compound were steep and narrow. Dennis dismounted, tied his horse to the corral fence, and dusted off his pants and shirt with his hat. There was dust in every wrinkle of his skin and clothing.

"Whatcha got to say, Angus?" Rusty said. "Howdy, ma'am."

When they pulled up, Angus was standing at the

door with a rifle in his white-knuckled fists. Green Leaf, his Crow wife, cowered behind him.

"It's all right, Angus. The danger is over," Dennis said. "We had a bit of trouble down the mountain, and this boy got shot bad. Let's get him inside and see if we can try to patch him up."

"What was all the shootin' about?" Angus asked. "It sounded like a war down there. I figured I'd stay up here and guard the cabins. That and protect the missis, my horse, and my mule."

"You wouldn't believe us if we told ya." Levi laughed. Looking back, what had happened seemed almost comical. "Somehow, these three fine specimens of human beings got both the Sioux and the Crow after 'em simultaneously. Levi here was hiding in the shadows watching the whole thing, and nobody ever noticed he was there. He's a crafty one, he is."

"So, why didn't you warn us of what you saw?" Ely grumbled. "Iffin you knew they were there, you were a fool not to give us fair warning."

"You call me a fool one more time, I'm gonna cut your tongue out," Levi snarled. He had found that lately when his temper got the best of him, he quickly jumped to anger. "Go ahead, call me a fool again, and see what happens."

"For some reason, you think you're stuck here with us, when in reality, we're stuck here with you," Rusty growled. "We'll take care of your brother, but you two can sleep with the animals. And if you happen to get any wild ideas about our mules and horses, we hang horse rustlers around here. The same as if you were caught in any city."

"And who was it that made you the law?" Ely snapped, his voice full of disdain.

"I made me the law," Rusty Steel replied as he locked eyes with Ely. Ely couldn't hold the stare. He flinched and averted his eyes. "If you or your brother wanna challenge me, I'll be happy to oblige."

# GUNSHOT WOUND

GREEN LEAF KNEELED, SO HER EYES WERE LEVEL WITH THE wounded man's. She put her hand on his face and frowned. She raised his lip to look at his gums. He was missing a half dozen teeth, and his mouth smelled terrible. She wrinkled up her nose and removed the rags stuffed into the wound, though she showed no shock or surprise. Perhaps she had seen things as bad and worse in her life with the Crow Indians. They were constantly at war with other tribes. Of course, there were the occasional treaties, but they were never upheld. Battle for land and bison were the order of the day, and things hadn't changed for centuries other than the arrival of the first horses.

The Spanish explorers and conquistadors brought horses to the North American continent. When the Indians ran the Europeans off and made them leave, in their panic to flee, they left their horses behind. For decades, they ran wild in the wilderness. Some adapted, evolved with their environment, and survived the land in the New World like they did in the Spanish countryside. Others perished like many animals in America. It was the survival of the fittest, even for mammals like horses. A pack of wolves could take a lone horse down in seconds. A grizzly bear could knock a horse down with one slap on the head.

In the same way, Christopher Columbus's arrival to the New World also changed the course of things. He and his shipmates were to change history by being the first foreigners on the American continent for ten thousand years. Except for the profound change in the discovery of horses, it was the most essential evolution in North and South American history.

Eventually, they became wild herds of horses and made their way across the country. The Plains Indians adopted them, changing their lifestyle for the first time in thousands of years. They mounted horses and fought and hunted their enemies and buffalo. This gave them the capacity to carry more of what they needed. It also allowed them to travel faster and flee quicker. Their world changed, and the Comanche dominated the tribes with their horsemanship skills and their will to fight.

At the time, the Spanish didn't know it, but they had reformed the future of the North American Indians for life. Even then, there was resentment toward Columbus by the Indian Nations for calling them Indians. This was due to the fact he had no idea where he was, believing he had found the passageway to India. Due to his mistake, the name *Indian* stuck for centuries. Unfortunately for the North American Indians, more changes were to come, and they weren't in any way beneficial to the tribes.

The warriors were very independent and often

started conflicts needlessly. But their way of life was war; without it, they were nothing. The Plains Indians weren't like the Cherokee in the East, who welcomed the White man and traded for their goods. They were clever and avoided conflict. But they didn't live off the buffalo as the Plains Indians did.

They weren't of the nomadic tribes that followed the buffalo to exist. That was what White men didn't understand. It would be like taking all their water. Then how could they survive? Tribes had lived in these lands for thousands of years, and it had always been the same. They were tribes of warriors with warriors' codes, and they lived off the buffalo that covered the plains.

Green Leaf expertly cleaned the jagged skin from around the hole in the right side of his chest with a sharp skinning knife. It appeared to enter just over his organs and through a lung. She could hear him gasp when he breathed, and he had blood in his mouth. She used her finger to fish around in the wound to make sure part of the bullet wasn't left behind. Sure enough, she found a piece of lead. It had lodged in a rib, stopping it from causing further damage. She sewed up the hole with a wildcat gut.

Then, with the help of the brothers, they turned Elroy over. The hole in his back was three times the size of his front. A large pool of blood covered the bed where he lay. She quickly cleaned the exit wound and poured some spirits in to wash away the blood and dead skin. It was good that Elroy was out cold, or he would have had to endure excruciating pain. When she was done, she put a large-bladed knife into the coals of the fire and sprinkled a gray powder into the wound. Green Leaf removed the knife when the blade's tip was glowing orange. She used it to sear the skin together as she squeezed the wound closed.

When she was done, she had claret up to her elbows. If anyone could save him up in the Rocky Mountains, it was Green Leaf. She also told fortunes for the people of her tribe. They were not poor, and she was paid handsomely for her services. Of course, even though she offered to try to cure the young man, she would still expect a gratuity. Angus usually made sure they paid up. Today wasn't any different than any other for him. She toiled over the damaged body for hours, and he decided how much she would get paid for her services. Of course, when she cured Crow Indians, the payment was different. Angus didn't get involved, and Green Leaf knew how to fend for herself with the Indians. They both knew White men always cheated Indians, though. This time, like others, he was there to ensure they didn't. From the Indians, this payment could come in the form of a box of eggs or a fat turkey. It depended on what the Indians could afford.

Finally, she cleaned off all the blood and washed her face. She lit several pieces of eucalyptus bark. The smell filled the room and smoke squirreled from the cinders. With several eagles' feathers, she pushed the smoke into Elroy's face and body. She chanted in some language, but it wasn't Crow. Dennis and Rusty didn't understand a word she spoke. They thought perhaps she was talking in tongues. She was surely speaking to the Crow spirits to save his life or protect him as he passed to the other side.

This went on all day long and into the night. Eventually, Green Leaves lay on the floor next to the wounded White man. She curled up in the fetal position and fell straight to sleep. Elroy was teetering between life and death. Throughout the night, she awoke, bathed his face in cool water, and made him drink. His body was soaked with sweat as the fever set in. Now his chances were even slimmer.

The two Grimms brothers took charge of watching Elroy. Neither wanted him to die on their watch. Sam, Bob, and Pete still looked at the elder Grimms brother with distrust. Ely didn't do anything to encourage one to trust him. He seemed as slippery as a snake. Now that they had them in their home, they had better make the rules clear and fast.

"Iffin y'all are gonna stay here, you can sleep in the last stable," Rusty said. "That means the both of ya. The young fella can sleep in the bed where he lay."

"You sure are an onery old cuss, ain'tcha? What happened to manners in a man?" Ely retorted. "Somebody should teach you a lesson, you old fool."

The older Grimms brother didn't see this one coming until it was too late. He caught the image of a massive fist in his peripheral vision as it closed in on his temple with lightning speed. When the bone-crunching punch landed on the side of his head, it wobbled a little like a broken hinge, but he didn't go down. Instead, he did the crazy walk as he continued to use every bit of strength to stay upright. Finally, it was more than his brain could take. His legs folded up under him like an ironing board, and he landed hard on the ground.

Levi drew back to give him another hot kiss at the end of a wet fist, but Forrester grabbed the six-foot-seven giant before he tore Ely's head right off his neck.

"Take it easy, pard," Forrester said. "You're gonna kill

'em if you hit 'em again. Take a few deep breaths and count to ten. He ain't worth the trouble."

Levi knew he had lost control of his temper again. It was something that happened more frequently as time passed. He wondered if he was changing into a man he didn't like. Of course, the three buffalo hunters were guilty of crimes of humanity and probably a few of the All Mighty too, but sometimes you needed to put a stop to disrespect. This let them know they better watch their manners around the mountain men.

"Are ya gonna sit there all day," Earnest spat, "or are ya gonna come with me to the stables? The way you've been actin', I'm surprised they even let us sleep with their mules, you dad-gummed fool."

Ely remained on the floor with his head in his hands. It was all he could do to stay conscious. He was surprised he didn't go straight down but remembered how his legs had turned to rubber, and he couldn't stand any longer. He had never been punched so hard in all his years of sassing people. He just realized these mountain men were up a notch or two above him and his brothers. They were much more challenging than they appeared. That was something he would have to remember in the future, or the same thing would happen again—maybe something even worse than what he had already experienced.

"I told ya not to call us fool again, moron," Levi spat. "When you can walk, get your butt out and over to the stables. I've seen enough of ya for one day. Earnest, give your brother a hand and get him out of here. He's wet himself and all. Maybe he'll treat us with a little more respect next time he opens his mouth. Either that or stay in the dad-gummed stables where we can't hear his sass."

Earnest struggled to get Ely up. Out of patience, Levi grabbed him by the scruff of his shirt and pulled him entirely off his feet. He shook him like a rag doll until you could hear his teeth chatter, then he turned him around.

"Open the door, Angus," Levi growled.

Then he kicked him in the butt and out the door, and Ely went tumbling off the porch. He lay there in the yard, face down. When Earnest walked by, he didn't even look at his brother. It appeared like he had had a good dose of his sass too. The mountain men all watched from the porch. After fifteen minutes or so, Ely struggled to his feet and wobbled for a moment. Then he got his bearings and headed for the stables. He zig-zagged across the yard, making anything but a straight line.

Once he staggered to the stables, Levi said, "I don't trust that Ely any farther than I can throw him."

"Why, what in the world did he do other than talk too much?" Forrester said. "Who knows what's going around in his head? You had your fun with that. Why don't cha leave it at that?"

"For a military man, sometimes you're too affable, Bill," Levi said. "You just watch. We ain't seen the last of the antics of those two rascals. I doubt the wounded boy be a problem if he lives. He didn't seem the type, but the middle brother is wishy-washy and could go either way. I reckon, in the end, he'd have to follow his big brother. That's how families be. Ely will only see what he lost in furs and horses. He might even be thinkin' about getting even. We still got the gold coins from the Rendezvous."

"They don't know nothin' about that," Forrester said.

"I agree," Rusty added. "How would they know about the money? But that don't mean he won't try to steal our furs. We've already got a good supply of hides left over from last winter that didn't get cured in time for the Rendezvous. They probably blame us for interloping in their affairs and all. We just spoiled their plans, and we be the only ones with something worth money. It don't take a scientist to figure it out."

"There's eight of us plus Green Leaf, so we've got plenty of eyes to spy on the two," Levi said. "I don't know if this boy on the bed will pull through. He's been unconscious for a good spell again. He may never wake up. At least we don't have to keep an eye on him."

# ELY GRIMMS

ELY STAGGERED INTO THE BARN WHERE THE STABLES WERE located. He stumbled along like he was dead drunk. His head was still spinning from Levi's blow. He had to hold on to the door for a minute to catch his breath. Thunder drummed between his ears, and he'd lost his hearing on his left side. He felt like a sledgehammer had hit him. It came so fast that he barely caught sight of the giant mountain man's fist just before it connected with his head.

At first, everything went black, and he nearly went out, but he could barely shake away the cobwebs of his mind and think straight. He moved his tongue around his mouth and found a loose tooth. He nudged it again, and it clattered onto the floor. It felt like his ear was plugged with something and constantly rang.

"Why, you're bleedin' from your ear, Ely," Earnest said, shocked. "Is that part of your brains seepin' out?"

"You're dumber than a piece of wood," Ely spat. "Your brains don't come out your ears. You say some of the stupidest things."

The smell of the barn, horses, and mules was trapped in the building, along with the odor of manure and straw. The owners had locked everything down as soon as they realized Indians were in the area. The first thing they would usually do was steal the horses if they found it wasn't too tricky. The eight mules protested as soon as the odd-smelling strangers entered their space. The horses groaned, and one even screamed and kicked on her stable door. Apparently, they didn't like the strangers.

The Grimms brothers stopped at the last stable. It was free of horses or mules, and the stall's floor was covered in hay. There were a couple of wooden boxes to sit on. A lamp hung beside the last stall at the end of the stables. At least they could see.

Ely pulled out a tobacco pouch and sprinkled some into a piece of paper. He twisted it tight and popped it into his mouth. He fished a match out of his pocket, scratched it on the wall, and puffed it to life. He blew the match out, broke it in two, and threw it on the floor.

"You best watch smoking in a barn full of hay," Earnest said. "You might burn the building down."

It was as if a light went on in Ely's mind. Of course, burning the barn was drastic, but it would be an excuse to let the animals out and spirit them away while the mountain men were battling the blaze. Why hadn't he thought of it before? It was a perfect distraction. This time, he knew he was on to something good. Sure, some of his plans didn't work out well, but most of his ideas were brilliant. He didn't realize he was the fool of all fools. He believed he was brilliant when he was the dumbest of the three. The only reason he got away with what he did was because he was the eldest brother.

"Hot diggity-dog! I've got a whopper of an idea! She's a doozy," Ely said. "I just figured out how we're gonna steal all their furs. We're gonna have to get our guns back too. If we don't leave Levi and his bunch any horses, they'll have to walk to follow us. It'll be a piece of cake. I doubt they even take chase with winter comin' and all. What are they gonna do? Follow us on foot?"

"But what about Elroy?" Earnest asked. "We can't abandon our brother."

"We'll give 'im a few days to rest, and then we'll set the barn on fire. We can say it was just an accident. Then we'll act like we're savin' the horses, but we'll be stealin' 'em instead. By then, Elroy should be able to sit on a horse. He's gonna have to buck up and be a man."

"Horse theft is a hangin' offense, Ely. You don't wanna get hung, do ya? I don't think we should push Elroy, either. Don't cha see he's teeterin' on the edge of life and death?"

"Didn't you hear what Rusty said?" Ely replied. "He said there ain't no law at all up here but them, and they ain't gonna be quick enough to catch us. I can guarantee ya that. So don't go worryin' about gettin' hung. Keep your eyes on the target; we'll come out of this better than ever. We'll have more furs and pelts than ever and fine horses to go with 'em. Once we leave these mountains, they'll never figure out where we've gone."

"Well, I don't know. It seems kind of sketchy to me," Earnest huffed. "It seems like we're breakin' the law or somethin'."

Earnest brought the horses several buckets of water, finally leaving the trough in the corner full. He brushed the animals down and checked them for injuries. It was a miracle one of them didn't get killed or at least struck with an arrow. He reminded himself to check on the horses later in the day.

Earnest was a kindly soul. He ran with his brothers only because he believed his influence would one day change them. He was a religious man too. All three had been as boys. Their ma made them go to church, but soon Ely gave it up. Elroy could go either way. He looked up too much to his older brother. He knew his brother was no good, but he was his flesh and blood. He had no choice but to try to keep them out of trouble. It was funny how Earnest never noticed that he never kept them out of trouble. Most of the time, his older and younger siblings got him into trouble. Still, he felt it was his life's calling—looking after his brothers so they didn't go too far and break one of the rules of the Almighty.

If Ely's middle name *was* trouble, his nickname was bad luck. He always had many plans, but he never got anything right. And, of course, his two brothers went with him when he got into trouble. He was one of those guys who were convinced they had everything planned out to the detail, but although he did do the leg work, his deductions were regularly wrong. One out of three ventures made them enough money to carry on, but the other two were always complete failures.

When they'd decided to go on a hunt for bison, Earnest was against it. He knew they would be in danger in Indian country, and he had heard the buffs were becoming more and more challenging to locate. When they finally found the buffalo, after weeks of searching, they shot and skinned plenty and were happy with how the season panned out. They had their hides stacked high on the backs of mules. Only to be taken away from the people they ran off the killing fields. So what? They only took potshots at them and didn't try to take a bead. They didn't kill anybody, and they were making it out to sound like they had committed some crime for killing the giant dumb beast. Everybody was doing it.

"I swear I'm gonna get even with that young pup if it is the last thing I ever do," Ely spat. It even hurt when he spoke because he felt like his jaw was hanging on by a broken hinge. "How dare he talk to me that way. I've never allowed anyone to speak to me in such a tone of voice. Who the heck does he think he is, a king?"

"Didn't you hear what they just said about you sassing 'em again?" Earnest asked, shocked his brother still entertained thoughts of revenge. "These folks look far too dangerous to tangle with, brother."

"When you find yourself in front of a bull, you don't go tackle him head-on, do ya now?" Ely said. "You look to somehow get behind 'em or distract 'em so we can steal all those beaver pelts and buffalo hides—at least as many as we can stack on the mules. It still won't cover what the Indians stole, but it'll help. Maybe we should be chasing them Crow. There weren't but a few left after the gun battle. If we find 'em, we get all our furs back and the hides we steal from here too. That's what we'll do, all right. After we skedaddle out of here, we'll go lookin' for the Crow. I reckon if we can find a herd of buffalo, we should be able to find a couple of Sioux hunters. We can hunt down those Sioux who stole our horses when we're done."

"Why do ya wanna steal iffin we're gonna take back our buffalo hides from them Crow Indians?" Earnest asked. "We ain't that hard up. If we chase the local

Indians around, we're bound to get kilt. They ain't easy like White men."

"Don't let that big lump of lard fool ya," Ely said, but his voice didn't sound as brave as he had hoped. "The bigger they are, the harder they fall, and that one is gonna fall mighty hard when I get my chance. I don't let nobody treat me like that."

"Maybe you ought to listen to what he said, and you won't end up deaf in two ears," Earnest huffed. "Sometimes I think you are a fool, brother, no offense. He's clobbered ya twice already, and you're ready for some more? I must admit, you've got more morale than I'll ever have. I would have stopped with the backhand. The side of your face is already turning purple. I've never seen a man hit so hard."

"I counted eight horses and eight mules in the stables on the way in, plus ours," Ely said. "We've gotta figure out how to get twenty-two critters out of here without them fools finding out. All we need is a half day's start. No White man can run that fast. Maybe we'll get lucky, and they'll fall off a cliff. All I know is I ain't leaving here until we've got what was taken from us. I figure the root of all our evil is in that fella they call Levi. They say he was the one who stole the horses from the Indians in the first place; then he let 'em go. Go figure that one out. Nobody gives away horses. There's somethin' fishy goin' on with that one."

"The one that punched ya?" Earnest asked. "You plan to pick him out and get your face bashed in again? As it is, one side's bigger than the other with the swelling. You're going to be a mess by the time it goes black and blue. I know you're always sayin' how book smart ya are and all, but don cha think gettin' beat up again is kind of stupid?"

"Shut your trap, will ya," Ely said. "All that comes out of your mouth are negative thoughts. I need some peace and quiet to think this through. I've still gotta figure out how to get away with the horses before we're discovered. I reckon first, we best get our guns. I just know the rest of the plan is there. It's on the tip of my tongue."

"We really ain't ever broke the law before, have we, Ely?" Earnest asked. "I don't like the idea of doin' something so illegal that they might hang us for it."

Ely didn't hear a word he said, though. His mind was deep in thought of exactly how it would work. He had to think of everything, every eventuality. Then he remembered his wounded brother. It gave him cause to pause. Did he really care if he took him with him? He would be a hindrance for weeks if he lived. Would he survive if they took him with them? Ely Grimms had never considered abandoning one of his brothers. They had done everything together since he could remember, and he was their big brother.

He was always there when they were young. Now they were grown, and he didn't see them with the same eyes as before. Either they had changed when they grew up, or Ely had been the one who had changed. It had been so gradual none of them had noticed, but they all had changed in many different ways, as children do when they become men.

Ely believed Earnest spent too much time reading the Bible. That was why he was so hesitant to commit a crime. He was always talkin' about fire and brimstone. Elroy wasn't the brightest light in town, but he did as he was told. That went a long way. Then there was the fact that they had the same blood running through their veins. Then again, maybe it was time to pull up roots and be on his way. His brothers were grown adults and could make their own choices. It would be more effortless living if he were alone.

Then he could keep all the money from the furs for himself. If they really didn't want any part of it, maybe Ely would oblige them both. That is, if his youngest sibling lived, which was looking unlikely. It might all work out easier than he thought. The idea of burning the barn down to steal the horses was brilliant. Now, all he had to figure out was how to get their guns out of the cabin without the mountain men knowing it.

Then another brilliant flash came to him. Maybe he could act like his brother Earnest said. He could act real nice and get their trust; then they would give them their rifles back if they said it was to go out and hunt. They would never expect them to be willing to leave their younger brother behind. Now, he had almost all the plan worked out, and he had no doubt it would go without a hitch. All he had to do was put on his friendly face and be as pleasant as pumpkin pie. First, he would have to pay more attention to his winged brother, Elroy. He didn't want them to think he had a cold heart. Not just yet, anyway.

# INDIAN REVENGE

THE CROW WARRIOR HACHTA SAT DEEP IN THE SHADOWS where light didn't penetrate. He was watching the mountain men's cabin from a safe distance. He was friends with Rusty Steel, but his hatred for buffalo hunters was more than he could stand. His people heard the story quickly due to the proximity of their camp and the cabins. If they didn't kill the White hunters, more would come and do the same as they had on the plains in Montana. The buffalo sought refuge in the harder to reaches stretches of the mountains and valleys. The survival instinct pushed them to hide even if they weren't aware of their actions. Now, he and his warriors sought revenge.

They already knew how dangerous the buffalo hunters were, but they still desired restitution for the men who had attempted to shoot them. They had also lost two of their best hunters when they led them to the Sioux warriors. When you try to kill an Indian, you must be held responsible for your actions, especially when it was a White man against a Crow hunter. Hachta had no intention of allowing this to pass despite his friendship with Rusty Steel. He would have to figure out a way to kill the three men who shot at his hunting party and ran them off the herd of buffalo. He had seen what was left after they had gone. Hundreds of bloody red carcasses covered the valley floor, contrasting with the green grass.

"I know I wasn't there, but I want you to follow my direction," Hachta said to his warriors. "If these White men tried to kill you, we must get revenge, or they will all begin to take shots at us whenever they want. There is no White man's law against shooting Indians. We are like wild animals to them, and they kill us for their trophies. They have 54-caliber long-guns specially made for shooting large animals from long distances. This was their secret weapon. Because of this and the sharp-shooters' precision, they were forced to flee the valley full of buffalo. By the time they returned, the buffalo were gone. They all know the story and what happened afterward. Now is the time to make a wrong, right."

"No one will be sad for the loss of these three White men," Blue Feather said. "It looks like one is almost dead anyway. The other one is so indecisive that I doubt he struggles much. The angry one will fight the hardest, but he, too, will lose. They have no chance once they are alone again. We only need to get close enough; their long rifles are not the right weapon. If possible, we should fight close enough for knives, and if not, then with arrows."

"I must wait, so I don't dishonor an old friend," Hachta said. "Rusty Steel and I go back a long time. He is a man you should beware of. You are young, and he is old and wise. Don't let his age trick you. He could kill you so swiftly that you won't know it until you're in the spirit world. I want us to be silent because I don't want to fight Rusty Steel and his friends. Then we may all die, and I don't want to destroy our friendship. He is the only White friend I have."

"I know we need to be patient, and they will come to us," Blue Feather said. "I know their leader of the hunters is a wicked man too. I could see the corrosion around his eyes. It went all the way to his soul. The gods will look down on us with their blessing for killing such an evil man."

"But we have the buffalo skins," Black Hawk said. "Why do we have to risk our lives again when we've got what we came for? I find it a needless risk of life. Haven't we lost enough already?"

"Some things are sacred, brother," Hachta said. "Our buffalo is one of these things. What would happen if White men came and killed all our buffalo? Then what would we eat, and where would we sleep? What would we use to cover us at night or make our coats? Our buffalo are sacred and must be defended, or more White men will come and wipe them all out."

"That's impossible," Blue Feather retorted. "The herds are so vast an Indian can run from horizon to horizon and never touch the ground."

"The word is, were...the herds *were* so vast, but now they are not," Hachta said. "I have not seen such numbers for three years. Sometimes, we have to search for weeks to find buffalo. They are already dwindling in size, and we see more hunters daily on the plains. These are the first ones to our valley, but when they have nothing left to hunt, they will come here to search. We must kill every man who hunts bison for money."

"And what about this friend of yours, Rusty Steel?" Blue Feather asked. "He, too, kills buffalo."

"Yes, but they only kill what they need for food and to make coats and blankets—the same as we do. They will never trap out their springs or over-hunt our forests. Rusty is a wise man and thinks more like an Indian than a White man. He has been through many things in his life. They said when he was a boy, he was a thief. Now he is a man of respect and honor. We must tread lightly, so we don't insult him or his friends. They, like us, have become part of the mountains. Remember, the mountains don't belong to us—we belong to the mountains."

They saw when one of the buffalo killers headed for the stables to be followed by the older one a little later. He appeared drunk as he staggered across the yard and to the barn while he held his head in his hands. He disappeared into the stables. The wounded man never left. They assumed he was still alive, or they would have removed the corpse from the house. Hachta didn't want any trouble with the eight men who lived in the compound. All he wanted were the three men who looked like brothers with red hair and noses as flat as shoes.

———

As the Sioux warriors rode through the forest, the bodies were on their mounts' backs. Dark Horse was among the dead. He had done everything he could to return to his tribe with the animals. All he'd wanted was to see his wife and infant son. At least Chaska would find out he fought bravely and had given his life at his request. He was dead, but his honor was intact. He did return with the stolen horses, though, but he now lived in the spirit world, and the dead body across the back of his horse was no longer the Sioux warrior Dark Horse.

Rain Man and Raven were the only survivors of the original war party. The rest were killed in the battle with the White hunters and the Crow Indians. They still didn't understand how it all happened. It would remain a mystery for everybody but a chosen few. Destiny had brought the four elements together in a violent clash. Of course, nobody expected such a thing. The laws of the universe had gone askew.

Now was the time to seek out the men responsible and make a wrong right. The buffalo hunters were their primary targets because they ended up with their animals, so they were horse thieves. The other man responsible was the White mountain man they called Levi Beaver Johnson. The Indians simply called him Beaver.

They got their horses back, which was their war chief's demand. Chaska was appalled at his actions when he was informed of the dangerous journey it took them on, especially for the loss of Dark Horse. All he had wanted was to see his wife and young child again, but it wasn't meant to be due to the war chief's orders. Now they were all in mourning, and the war Chaska felt the weight of knowing he'd sent men needlessly to their deaths. Sometimes leaders had to make hard decisions, though.

Chaska wondered once again how sound his orders

were. He knew he ruled his band of warriors with an iron fist, but he felt he was always fair and never asked anyone to do something he wouldn't do himself. Perhaps what he considered reasonable was already a step too far in the wrong direction. He walked to where Dark Horse's wife wailed. She was beside herself with grief. A papoose was tied to her back. His son was too young to understand, but the elders would tell stories of his bravery. Chaska wondered if the songs sung after his death would be kind or cruel. He pushed the thought into the dark corners of his mind. It was dangerous for war chiefs to think about such things.

He knew he had to show his respect and carry on like every day when his heart bled for his friend. Right then, he made a promise to himself. He would care for Dark Horse's son like he was his own, especially now that he didn't have a father. He would try to be the father he had denied him with his reckless order. The scrubby horses weren't worth it. Yet, there they were, just like he had demanded. Any little victory he might have felt was wiped away by their losses.

Sometimes in the heat of the moment before a battle, a chief was sure some men would lose their lives. He reminded himself that Dark Horse went to the Rendezvous against his orders like six others. They also bought White men's whiskey, which he had made sermons against to all his tribe. He'd even forbade his warriors ever to taste their spirits. Yet the temptation of the unknown was more than his men could tolerate. Dark Horse had fallen asleep from White men's whiskey, and the mountain man they call Beaver spirited their horses away.

None of them knew how the horses went from the mountain men to the buffalo hunters. They assumed they must have been sold or possibly stolen. Most of it would remain a mystery to the majority. When he thought back on the plan, it made him frown. It was rife with holes and problems. He realized it was a desperate attempt to take land from men who had spent much of their lives struggling to survive there. Before, nobody wanted that land. At the time, he believed if they didn't claim it for his tribe, the Crow would eventually have it. Wild game was scarce everywhere these days, and the buffalo were quickly dwindling.

The tribe's chief, Black Cloud, saw the dilemma. The territory they had tried to claim wasn't precisely Sioux land, nor was it Crow. Until then, nobody wanted it or even claimed it due to its difficult location and complicated trails leading to and from. That was probably why the first White man built a cabin there more than ten years earlier.

That was also the reason nobody bothered them all this time. They lived like Indians but also had lots of guns, powder, and lead balls. They had long guns that shot as far as a man could see, and he knew the mountain man Rusty Steel had one.

He was the most known of the White men in the Rocky Mountains. For the first years, he lived alone and shunned all human beings. He became something of a curiosity for the Indians.

When he made friends and moved in with Mountain Dennis, the Indian tribes were happy enough to have them so far away. The Crow traded for goods the Indians needed but only White men had.

They had never caused trouble before the Sioux went there to run them off, take their traps, and hunt their game. White Weasel wondered if it was wise to bother the eight mountain men who lived in the cabins. He had heard they had Crow friends in the camp not a half day from the compound. They would have to wait to catch the giant White man when he was alone, possibly in the little smelly house behind the cabins where they went to read.

Now, Chief Chaska and White Weasel were again in charge of seeking out the White men. This time, they were after the buffalo hunters too. They were their biggest enemies, who needed to be eliminated immediately. If not, the buffalo would vanish. When they saw the three dead, they would focus their attention on Beaver.

They rode through the forest as quietly as possible. There were twenty warriors, the best men the tribe had. He knew they would have no protection back in camp if he lost them. He'd tried to reason with Chief Black Cloud, but he wouldn't budge from his decision. Of course, he hadn't lost one of his closest childhood friends. Nor had he made the order that brought him to his death. He had never even seen the land he proposed to claim.

He wondered what Black Cloud really wanted. He didn't see him sending out his best men against such formidable fighters unless it was more than simple revenge. The Indian way was complicated and even more so for the chiefs and war chiefs.

Every order they made put men in peril, and sometimes things didn't appear to be what they were. He couldn't help but feel it was still about the land.

The chief knew that if they wanted to kill Beaver, they would have to go through Rusty Steel and his band of misfits. It wouldn't be easy, but if they did pull it off, their chief would be sung about in song, and it would push their territory even closer to the Crow. With luck, one day they would push them out.

# THICKER THAN
# WATER

IT WAS A LAZY AFTERNOON IN THE COMPOUND. WHITE clouds floated across the bright blue sky like puffs of cotton. Birds sang in the trees as cicadas chattered. The mountain men had had a busy morning, but with good collaboration and the added help of Green Leaf, they'd finished their daily chores early. Now they had time to have a smoke and maybe even a drink and tell some stories or tales—perhaps even a few lies. The smell of freshly perked coffee floated on puffs of air soon to be mixed with the scent of sweet tobacco. Tomorrow was Sunday, and as a rule, Dennis respected the Sabbath.

Years before, when Rusty arrived, it was already a habit. His inclusion into the group of rugged men didn't change their customs, even though Steel was from the other side of the coin. As a boy, he was a beggar and a thief. He knew how hard life could be, so it was difficult for him to believe everything from God was good. He thought the world was populated with primarily honest people, but there was a good dose of evil too. Most of these wicked folks seemed to gravitate to lands with no law or were fleeing from a Wanted poster. This pushed them west of the big eastern cities and east of civilization on the Pacific Ocean. Somewhere between Old Fort Boise and Kansas City, men made their own laws.

Dennis had come from a family schooled in religion, but Rusty was different, even though he saw the logic in giving a man a day off. The struggle in the mountains was hard on any level. They had to trap waist-deep in freezing rivers and springs, fight grizzly bears, mountain lions, and packs of hungry wolves. Then they had the constant threat of hostile Indians, which wasn't all that Mother Nature threw at them. There were also blizzards where they could be snowed in for weeks and whiteouts where you couldn't see your hand before your face.

Then again, the beauty of the Rocky Mountains outweighed the problems for those few who chose to live the life of a mountain man. It also provided the constant challenge for which such men lived. If it was easy, they wouldn't be interested. It was the difficulties that lured many, that and the unknown. If a man sought out excitement, Mother Nature, and challenges, then this was the life for him. If you weren't up to the mark, you would fail utterly. Only the hardest managed to survive in such hostile environments. Often failure led to death. Others saw it was too much for them and quickly ran with their tails between their legs. They were the lucky ones who survived long enough to flee.

Green Leaf was fussing over Angus as usual. She was checking his hair for lice. He was so tall and she so short, she stood on a chair to reach his scalp. The gangly man purred like a kitten from the attention. The question the group of mountain men had was how in the world did he do it—something they asked themselves daily. They had never seen a homely, gangly man get so much attention from the opposite sex. Of course, none knew if this was the same back in civilization. He had been a mountain man as far back as any men living in the compound could remember. At least among the Flathead and Crow women, he was considered quite a catch. They all agreed it had to be how he could cut it up when he danced.

Bill Forrester sat with his boots on the hitching post and his chair precariously pushed back. Levi sat at the edge of the porch playing mumbly-peg. Everybody sipped on coffee except Green Leaf, who slurped on a tea she made from roots. She used it to moisten Leroy's lips, who still lay in Forrester's bed. He was the lowest on the totem pole. Bill used his bedroll at night and curled up by the fire. The other two buffalo hunters spent their nights in the chilly stables and their days in the sun or on Rusty's porch. When they were present, the conversation was more guarded, like no one really trusted them. Lately, Ely was making futile attempts to befriend the men in the compound, but first impressions outweighed anything he might do to trick the pathfinders in the future.

The mortally wounded Leroy made a ragged hissing sound every time he breathed. Each one sounded like it was his last breath. It left everyone on edge, expecting it to be the final gasp. Then after what seemed far too long, he would gobble up some more air and start again. His windpipe rattled like a Persian blind. His face glistened with sweat as he shivered with cold. He had been like this for days, neither getting better nor worsening. Not once had he regained consciousness, not even for a moment. He seemed to be in limbo between the living and the dead.

It was good for Green Leaf to have a break from caring for the gutshot buffalo hunter. Nobody expected him to survive such a wound, and all the mountain men knew that if he did survive, he would have to be cared for weeks, if not months. The entry hole and exit wound inside his lung would heal slowly and had to be closed before he could travel. Each day, they expected to awaken to a silent room, but he continued to wheeze and whistle as he struggled to survive.

"He sure does have some go in 'im," Angus said as he shook his head. "That boy Elroy is as hard as nails. He should have died the first day with that hole in his back, but he won't give up. I reckon he still has some things on his bucket list he's trying to stick around to tend to."

"Where are his brothers?" Rusty asked suspiciously. "I think they're up to somethin'. I don't trust 'em enough to sleep in the house with us. That Ely looks to be the type to slit your throat in your sleep."

"Is that why you locked up so tight last night?" Forrester chuckled.

"That Earnest seems like a fine man," Dennis said. "I've seen him reading his Bible every morning. It pains me to see him sleep out in the stables."

"They have plenty of hay to keep warm with their bedrolls," Forrester said. "We don't all fit in here anyway unless we're in a pinch."

"Yeah, but that brother of his, Ely, ain't like him at all, and I'd say, despite his gravitation toward the right-eous, I reckon he'll do whatever his big brother says," Rusty said. "I can see in his eyes that he's up to somethin'. Every time I see 'em, he's grinnin' like a possum—like everything is fine and dandy. Earnest sits beside his wounded brother for hours and reads and prays for him. I don't see Ely give him more than a fleeting glance to see if he was dead or alive. He didn't seem to be bothered one way or the other. It was like he was impatient for something to happen."

"Ely wouldn't leave before his brother dies or gets better, would he?" Angus asked, shocked at the thought.

"I figure he may well leave 'im for us to look after, given half a chance," Levi said. "We've still got their rifles, don't we? I'm surprised they ain't insisted on gettin' 'em back, and their pistols too."

"They're locked up inside the gunrack, and their pistols are in the chest under lock and key," Rusty replied. "Unless they go over me, they ain't gonna be armed as long as they're here. From what Earnest said, they were already takin' pot shots at the Crow to run 'em off the buffalo herd. That's probably what brought 'em here in the first place. You can't shoot at Indians and expect them to forgive ya. They'll track ya halfway across the country if needed. They ain't the forgivin' kind."

"How in the world did the Sioux war party get mixed up into this?" Portland Pete asked. Before smallpox left a dozen small craters across his cheeks, he was a good-looking man. "These three must have found those horses you ran off the Sioux camp. You know—that war party that was plannin' on killin' us and throwin' us off the mountain. The Indians must have thought they were rustlers, but Levi didn't steal anything. I reckon they got the wrong men. He just ran 'em off to put 'em a foot, hopin' they would give it up, but that didn't work out, now did it?"

"I reckon they should take care of Elroy at least," Levi said. "I doubt he's twenty years old. He seems too young to die. Iffin they leave 'im here, I know it would be a burden, but I can't see turning a dying man away."

"Well, I'm glad you volunteered because I ain't got the time. We're not talkin' about dying here, anyway," Rusty said. "We're talkin' about livin'. I'm afraid part of stayin' alive is keepin' an eye on the oldest Grimms because he's got something planned. They lost their summer hides and might get the bright idea to take ours. We can return their weapons when we see them mounted on their horses and ready to ride down the mountain. Until then, they'll be more manageable iffin they ain't armed."

"Remind me you said that a month from now." Dennis chuckled. "We're all gonna get tired of this situation real quick. I can't say I'd like those two sleepin' in our barn that long. I know they don't wanna go home empty-handed even though it was them that got the Crow after 'em."

"I was the one that ruffled the Sioux's' feathers, though," Levi said. "They took them for the ones who stole their horses even though I ran 'em off."

Ely and Earnest walked out of the barn and headed for Rusty's porch. They all gravitated there in the afternoon as it was twice the size of the porches on the other two cabins. Every eye turned their way, with Ely grinning like a Cheshire Cat the whole time. Earnest's furrowed brow and sad eyes showed his concern for his younger brother. It looked like the older brother had all but forgotten about him. They all knew any man who turned his back on his own kin was no good.

"Morning, gentlemen," Ely said with a smile, but it didn't reach his eyes. "Is there any chance to get some of that coffee I smell?"

Earnest didn't say a word as he rushed for the door and to the bed of his dying brother. The blood drained from his face when he saw his state. He was losing weight fast, and unconscious, they could only squeeze a towel over his mouth, so drops of water passed his parched and cracked lips. He hadn't eaten for days.

Levi wiped his knife on his pants, slipped it back into his boot, and stood. The porch planks groaned under his weight. He went in to check on Earnest. He felt sorry for the man. He had never lost a close family member, so he really didn't know how he felt, but it bothered him just the same. Even though Levi was a giant and instilled fear in most, he also had a gentle and kind soul. He felt for the very Indians that wanted to kill him. Johnson was one of the few who understood the Indians' dilemma and was smart enough to stand back and see the whole picture.

---

EARNEST SAT beside the window where the morning light shined into the stables. He sat on a pile of hay and leaned against the wall. His finger followed the words as he read from his Bible like he did every morning. The sun on his freckled face made him seem like a young boy for just a moment. Unlike his older brother, he was an innocent soul. Ely walked over and nudged him with his boot. There was more than a bit of anger in the touch.

"Ouch!" Earnest barked, surprised. He had been engrossed in his reading.

Ely looked around to ensure nobody else was in hearing distance and whispered, "I figure today's the day we set the barn on fire. I've been friendly with that ornery bunch of misfits all week, and I think they're comin' around. Soon they'll be like putty in my hands. Nobody will see us if we set it on fire tonight. If they do, all we have to say is we're saving the animals. I need to look in the cabin again to see where they have our rifles and handguns. There's only one room, so they should be easy to spot. You can run with the horses, and I'll sneak into the cabin while the boys are busy tryin' to put the fire out. I'll take a mule to load the furs and skedaddle and catch up with ya. By the time they put the fire out, iffin they can, we'll be miles away and with all their horses. They'll never catch us by then."

Earnest looked at his brother, horrified. He was silent for a moment with his jaw on his chin. Finally, he recovered from the shock and said, "Are you thinkin' about leavin' before Elroy dies? I know as well as you he ain't gonna make it. Just because he doesn't come around and eat food has him on death's door. I can't leave my brother until he's passed on, though. I planned to bury him in a nice place I found in the woods. I was hopin' we'd wait until the end, then he wouldn't be breakin' any of the rules of the All Mighty before he headed for heaven. Iffin he goes with us, he'll be headin' for hell."

"Why are you always so dad-gummed dreary?" Ely spat. "You read too much of that book you cherish so. We ain't gonna kill anybody, so don't worry about it. All we're gonna do is get what's ours back again. It don't matter to me who took it. These scoundrels were the ones that gave our furs and horses away that we found fair and square. A Grimms can't let such a thing go unavenged. We ain't really doin' anything wrong iffin you look at the right way. Were it not for that Levi Johnson, we would have never had the Sioux after us, and we could have handled the Crow. They ain't nearly as ornery."

"I already said I'd go with ya, but I never said I'd leave before Elroy dies," Earnest said, his eyes pleading. "That just wouldn't be right."

Ely chewed on his bottom lip as the gears in his mind began to spin, and he searched for a way to get his hardheaded brother to go with him. He wanted to escape the mountain men before they discovered his true nature. He knew who and what he was and didn't have a problem with what kind of person he'd become. The only thing that had always hindered him was his two brothers. He always had them tagging along on every venture he made. Earnest was always complaining too, and Ely was fed up.

"Come on, you," Ely said as kindly as a snake. "Let's go drink some of those fools' coffee. Maybe they'll invite us to a biscuit too."

He wore a deep frown as his eyes narrowed, and he stared hard at Earnest. He didn't even return his brother's gaze. Maybe he already knew what he was going to see. As soon as he passed the barn door and walked into the sun, his bright and overly friendly smile stretched across his face again. His brother tore away as he headed for Elroy's bedside. Ely just managed to stifle a snicker. He had figured out the last bits of the puzzle. Now he had his plan.

He looked in the cabin door and walked over to where Earnest kneeled. His lips moved as he murmured something. Ely gave him a look of disgust. He thought his brother was weak, so he needed the crutch of religion.

He stood over Earnest and feigned sorrow. He put his hand on his brother's shuddering shoulders and whispered, "It'll be all right there, little brother. Why don't you go on outside for a spell? Don't let them hard men see you cry. I'll keep an eye on poor little Elroy here."

Earnest was embarrassed as he wiped away the tears with his shirt sleeve. He wiped his nose with his hand and blinked the drops from his eyes.

"Go out the side door, brother," Ely said. "You know how men be. They'll just make fun of ya."

He got up and struggled to hold back the sobs. His shoulders began to shake again as soon as he stepped outside. Ely shot a quick glance over his shoulder and to the porch. Then, using his body to block the view, he held his hand over Elroy's nose and mouth. It was so much easier than Ely expected; he found it curious, leaving him spellbound for a moment. It was the first life he took like that, all close and personal. You couldn't get more personal than killing your own flesh and blood. At least now he wouldn't have him holding everything up. Elroy's body racked and shuddered one last time, and he was gone.

He stood and looked back at the porch again. Nobody paid any attention to the two strangers. Then without a word, he followed his grieving brother as Elroy lay dead in the bed behind him.

"How ya doin' there, pard?" Ely asked, feigning concern. "Don't you worry now. Once he passes on, you'll get over all this. Even if you feel it's a struggle, life goes on, Earnest. It don't matter what we do. It ain't gonna change anything. Life be hard like that. Who knows, maybe he will get better all of a sudden."

Earnest looked up at his brother from where he sat. He was in the shadows leaning against the side of the cabin. He had stopped crying, but his eyes were red, and the tears had cut white paths down his cheeks.

"Do you really think he still has a chance to get better?" Earnest asked, hoping and praying his brother would say yes.

"Why, anything's possible, little buddy," Ely said, although the lie was in his eyes. They were still glazed over from the feeling of killing his own kin. "You just don't worry your head about that. Whatever God wants to happen will, and it'll be the right thing too. Ain't that what it says in the Bible? I believe it was: the Lord works in mysterious ways."

# HELL'S FIRE

THE SIOUX AND CROW INDIANS NEARED THE MOUNTAIN where they had the battle only a week before. Again, the constellations aligned, and the world was thrown askew. Despite all odds, the same people found themselves in similar yet very different situations. The only common factor was the hate for the buffalo hunters—the mountain men included. They all knew the cabins were there, but neither knew of the presence of the other.

The Crow wanted the lives of the buffalo hunters who shot at their men and stole their buffalo. With the Sioux, the objective was different. They, too, intended to kill the White men who killed buffalo and rustled their horses. They also wanted Levi Beaver Johnson's scalp, his friends dead, and all the land.

The Crow had ridden down to the northeast side of the compound and the Sioux up to the southwest. They arrived in the dark of night. They didn't want to get near the cabin until right before they attacked. Both war parties had similar plans. They would attack and kill the buffalo hunters. Then they would deal with Levi

Johnson. Only the Sioux warriors sought his death, and even they did so half-heartedly. They had seen the man; his size and skills had already made their way to the elders' songs. Chief Black Cloud also wanted his friends dead too. They were to destroy their homes and take over their string of traps in nearby springs. Although it was part of their plan, if it appeared too dangerous, they would abandon it before losing more lives. This time Chaska intended to lose no men. He would abandon the attack despite his orders if he saw it was too risky. As he lay there watching, he wondered what he was doing there.

They hid their horses and set out guards. This time, nobody was going to be stealing their animals. This was the night three buffalo killers, and the rest of the White men, were to die. Of the Sioux war party, only Chaska dared near the White men. He trusted no one else. He had seen how these men lived and survived in such hostile lands. He had no doubts about how tough they would be. He did have his doubts about the buffalo hunters. They were used to killing defenseless dumb animals from a safe distance.

These weren't warriors like the Sioux and the men who lived in the compound. To him, they were the scum of the earth. He wanted to feel their warm blood on his hands as he cut their throats. He got close enough to smell the tobacco and see the orange cinders glow in the dark. When an owner puffed on a pipe, the burning ember lit up their face.

Chaska saw Levi Johnson at the edge of the porch. He was bigger than he had remembered. He didn't like what they were sent to do, nor did his men, but orders were orders. To him, it made no sense. The mountain men had been honorable and returned their horses. The loss of life was of their own doing. It was a poorly executed attack combined with an awkward run-in with a Crow war party. The chief wanted to save face and again try to take land that belonged to no one. The only claimants were eight hardened Rocky Mountain men.

Still, Chaska knew if he broke the chain of command, the structure of their warriors would immediately fall apart. He had been indoctrinated in the order of the warrior. After much sacrifice, he'd become a war chief. He knew his chief was too proud, and his ego was far too big. Chaska hoped if the day came and he did become chief of their small tribe that he would be wiser and only send his men on missions he would be willing to go on himself.

Chief Black Cloud would never get caught near a battleground. It wasn't that he was a coward, but he knew how risky the life of a Sioux warrior was. Many had already died at the hands of White men—many for the vanity of a chief. It was the same in many tribes. Power did things to a man. Some were good, and others not so much.

On the other side of the cabins, Hachta was doing the same thing the Sioux were. He, too, made his men stay back. Rusty Steel was his friend, and he didn't want an eager warrior brave to jump the gun because he lacked the patience to wait for the right moment. He would prefer to draw the buffalo killers out if he could. He sat still as a stone and breathed in a deep breath of air. He identified the odors and scents of his surroundings. His brow furrowed when he smelled freshly turned dirt—the smell of death. It was as unmistakable as bear fat, which he had stopped using. He now knew the mountain men could smell that too.

———

EARNEST'S SHOULDERS shook again as he kneeled by the freshly dug grave of his brother Elroy. Ely stood beside his brother in his time of grief with his hand on his shoulder, but he had to force a smile off his lips. All the holdups were now past, and they had finally sent his little brother on his way. He already had one foot in the grave anyway, and Ely didn't feel remorse for helping him pass. He had convinced himself that there was no way Elroy would recuperate from the gunshot wound, even though he had survived a whole week before he smothered him.

Ely thought he would feel some hint of sadness, but he had already accepted Elroy's death when he saw the gunshot wound. Even then, he thought it was just a matter of time. He eliminated the suffering of his brother Elroy, and now he could get on with the rest of his plan. So far, it looked flawless.

It was funny how Ely kept doing the same thing repeatedly, expecting different results. Some said that was a sign of insanity. Whatever it was, he felt free after Elroy was in the ground. Now he had to figure out what to do with Earnest.

He struggled to keep the smirk off his face as Earnest said some last words and read a few verses from his Bible. Teardrops splattered on the coffin as the mountain men lowered the casket into the ground—six feet under. Earnest threw the first handful of dirt on the wooden box. As it hit the wooden top, it sounded final.

This was the end of the road for their little brother. Ely grabbed a handful and recklessly tossed it on the grave and turned to go. He had already had enough of the ceremony and had his daily lesson from the Bible provided by his brother, whether he wanted it or not.

"You can give me the shovel, Mr. Steel," Earnest whispered as he wiped his eyes with his shirt sleeve. "I feel it's my duty to bury him properly. If I could have a little privacy with my brother as I send him along to heaven, I'd be mighty obliged."

The men nodded, and with bowed heads, they turned back for the compound. The grave was a few dozen yards into the woods in a little natural clearing. Sun slanted through the leaves like rain. The yellow orb still shone brightly as it appeared to hang from a string over the horizon. Vultures lazily circled in the sky above. Today they would be cheated out of their meal. Finally, Earnest covered the grave with stones so the coyotes couldn't dig the body up and drag it into the woods to eat.

————

CHASKA CRAWLED to the edge of the woods about a hundred yards from the porch. That was where the mountain men gathered to smoke and pass the time. He could only see one of the buffalo hunters, the ones that took shots at his hunters and stole their herd even though it was Crow territory and they had arrived first. Later, everyone witnessed the death and destruction the three White men left. Only the vultures and scavengers profited from this wholesale massacre. Even though the buffalo hunters lost their hides, that didn't make what they did right. They were forced to by Rusty Steel, or they wouldn't have given up a single fur.

Chaska knew the White hunters would return next season and maybe even bring more men with them. Then there would be even fewer buffalo for them to hunt. If they allowed this to continue, they would vanish from the plains. They were still a proud nation, but the men in Washington were pounding them into the ground one buffalo hide at a time. They had to eliminate the White men and claim the land they lived on for the Sioux.

He crawled on his belly as close as he dared. He had covered his hair and buckskins in branches and leaves. He was aware of Rusty Steel's uncanny skills. He had both those of a White warrior and an Indian brave too. Chaska sniffed the air. He listened carefully for every sound. He had made sure he was downwind. He had heard the one named Dennis could tell a possum from a raccoon with his uncanny sense of smell.

That was when it hit him. It was the same smell of the Indians they fought the week before. He shook his head and immediately backed out of his hiding place and toward his warriors. Now he had to decide who was the bigger enemy, but this was an excellent opportunity to make sure the Crow didn't come to this part of the mountain. They would be close to their stronghold if they took over this land. Depending on the size of the Crow camp, they might have to move, but his orders were to capture the buffalo hunters first. These men Chief Black Cloud wanted to torture personally.

"Give me a match, Earnest. It's time to start the party," Ely said.

His brother's eyes were spread wide. He was scared to death. He took a gasp of air and nodded, too frightened to speak. He knew what he was doing wasn't right, but they did have their furs taken. By American law, they were in their rights. It appeared that in the Rockies, Washington's rules didn't apply.

"Get the stable doors open and start shooin' the mules and horses out," Ely whispered. "We'll take the whole lot. Slow and easy now. We don't want to make any noise and wake these fools up."

Ely grinned. Now he was happy. The final part of his perfect plan was in motion. In half an hour, they would be headed down the mountain, and the mountain men would be back at the compound fighting the fire. Even if they knew they did it, they would need all eight to put a barn fire out. It was a cinch to set the hay alight. The rest would spread on its own.

"Take the horses down the south trail, and I'll be right behind ya. Leave me one of the mules," Ely whispered as he grabbed the reins of his horse and a mule and turned for the dark cabin.

The clopping of horses' hooves could barely be heard in the dark. Despite his fear, Earnest managed to get the animals to move together down the narrow trail. It was a good choice because it would be harder for them to turn around if they decided to head back home. He was so nervous he had to remind himself to breathe. His mouth felt like it was stuffed with cotton balls. His hands were wet and slippery.

Ely waited around the side of the cabin in the shade of a sliver of moon. Flames from the stables reflected in the windows of the house. He held his ear to the thick timber wall but heard nothing. He needed them to wake up in a panic and run to save their barn.

The sound of the bell nearly made Ely jump out of his skin. It came from the middle cabin. A man stood on a small porch with his fist wrapped around a ship's bell rope. The shrill sound sliced through the night and bounced off mountains and canyons. It sounded like dozens of bells were ringing simultaneously as it echoed time and again.

Like Ely planned, the men in the cabin ran out the door like their hair was on fire. As soon as he counted eight silhouettes, he climbed into the window. He went straight for the rifle rack, grabbed a hammer by the door, and broke the padlock. He grabbed their rifles and two shotguns. He looked around, but he didn't see the pistols. The double barrels would work better were they forced to fight their way out. Even Ely was amazed at how well his plan was working.

He reached out the window and leaned the long guns against the wall; then, he threw bundles of nearly cured cold weather beaver pelts out the window. When he figured he had as much as the mule could carry, he tied them down and walked into the darkness. When Ely reached the edge of the compound, he mounted up and rode through the gate. He shot a glance over his shoulder and was surprised. The fire was nearly out; only part of the stables had burned. How could they have gotten so much water to the fire in time?

He suddenly felt the need to hurry. It would be minutes before they figured out what happened. Still, he knew he had made it. He was on horseback, and they were on foot. They would probably chase them for a while, but he planned to ride for two days and nights. They had plenty of horses to trade off to rest the tired animals. They had ridden such distances chasing buffalo in the past, so he knew they could do it. Once they rode hard for two days, there was no way the mountain men would catch up.

He saw Earnest up ahead, driving the horses down the narrow trail. He laughed out loud, and his brother shot a glance over his shoulder. Ely expected to see a smile, but he saw a frown instead. His brother was never happy. Ely gigged his horse and caught up, pulling up spur-to-spur with his brother.

He grabbed his coat, pulled him close, and whispered, "Good luck at the gates of heaven, little brother." Then he pushed the long thin knife between his ribs under his armpit, slicing straight into his heart. Earnest looked at his brother, puzzled, like he didn't understand what was happening. Ely watched as the light went out in his eyes. He tumbled off his horse, and the knife slipped out and remained in Ely's fist. Warm blood dripped from the tip, and the blade and his hand were covered in thick claret.

Ely suddenly felt like a weight had been lifted from his shoulders. Instead of being sad, he was happy. He started to sing a tune he had heard back in civilization. "Oh, Susana, don't you cry for me, because I come from Alabama with a banjo on my knee."

He remembered the nearly extinguished fire and wheeled his horse around to look, but nobody was there yet. He gigged his horse and bumped him up into a fast trot. He wanted to ride faster, but with one drover, it was hard to keep all the stolen horses moving at the same speed. He had never worked as a cowhand on a ranch and was surprised at how difficult it was, but he knew he was a fast learner. He also wanted to avoid a stampede which would cost him eleven horses and nine mules, all of which were quality animals. Then he had all those pelts. They still needed some work to fetch top dollar, but he wasn't lazy when it came to making money.

Ely struggled to keep the horses and mules in line when the trail widened.

*Maybe I should cut all the mules loose but the one with the pelts*, he thought.

With fewer and faster animals, he figured he would make better time. He didn't seem to be moving as fast as he had assumed he would. Then again, he had killed his brother in the spur of the moment. Sure, he had pondered it on occasion, but when he was still unhappy after successfully rustling a small herd of livestock and stealing a mule full of furs, he knew it was what he had to do. The furs were owed to them anyway, just like the horses. There weren't any laws in America against shooting at Indians either, and he was sure nobody saw him kill his brothers. Back at the cabin, everybody was so relieved Leroy had passed nobody asked questions. They had all expected it anyway.

If they wanted to come down to civilization and go to a court of law, Ely didn't mind. He knew what Rusty Steel did by giving his horses and hides away was against any White man's law. No court in the country would consider a White man taking a potshot at an Indian a crime. They didn't even kill anybody.

They did get to kill their buffalo, though, which was legal too. Ely smiled again. He knew he was in his rights. All he had to do now was make it back to civilization with all his valuables. Once he sold everything off, he figured he would head for San Francisco for a month or so. He was tired of living in the wilderness, sleeping rough every night.

———

WAR CHIEF CHASKA saw them first. It was a string of horses with empty saddles. Behind them came a line of mules. Then he saw one of the buffalo hunters riding drag on the little herd. He had to be patient until the other one showed. He knew they had buried the one with the gunshot wound the day before. It had taken him a week to die. It was a shame they didn't get to kill him too. When they captured the two, they planned to take days torturing them.

This would be done back in their camp so Chief Black Cloud could make the most of his victory. He wanted the buffalo hunters alive, but Chaska planned to take his scalp before they surrendered their prisoners. It would be a slow and excruciating death. Now they had walked right into their trap. The first part of the plan was accomplished without even an injury. Now there was no way out for the buffalo hunters.

Chaska had known from the start what his chief had asked of him was a monumental feat. He was to battle eight of the best fighters and shots in the Rocky Mountains, all without losing a man. It was impossible to accomplish, but just the same, those were his orders. If he saw the casualties were too significant, he would retreat. If they fought hard and were honorable warriors, nobody would look down on them for failing —nobody except the chief. He would probably send them out again to do the same thing, expecting a different result. It was a vicious cycle.

Then he saw the second rider bolt up to the first. Chaska's eyes narrowed as he focused on the images in the night. The brothers seemed to be talking, then one dropped off his horse. He didn't move and appeared to be dead. Then he heard the White man laugh. Chaska made the sound of a coyote, and his men closed in so quickly that the buffalo killer didn't know they were there until they pulled him off his horse. Little did they know Hachta and his Crow warriors were one step ahead of the Sioux. They too had followed the buffalo killer and he led them right to Chaska and his war party.

At that very moment, the night sky filled with arrows. Dozens fell in the first seconds. Chaska was among the first to be wounded. Then there were hundreds of stone-pointed projectiles falling like rain. The Sioux war party was distracted by the capture of their buffalo hunter. They forgot that in the wilderness, the unexpected was right around the corner. Arrows stuck out of everybody and everything. Six arrows protruded from Ely Grimms's body. He groaned as blood poured from his mouth.

Chaska had been luckier than most. He had two arrows in each leg. As the confusion continued, under cover of darkness, he crawled through the shadows of a silver sliver of moon. He pulled himself into the forest and dug his way into a bush. He buried himself as deeply as possible and lay as still as a stone.

He heard men speaking in Crow. It had been a surprise attack from the rear. He wondered if only he had survived. He knew this was madness, but it had turned out worse than ever expected. The Crow had made it clear this was their mountain, and the Sioux would have to relinquish their new claim. Chief Black Cloud would be very unhappy but not as unhappy as the wives and children of those lost.

If Chaska made it back to camp, he would tell the story, and the tribe could pick a new chief. Black Cloud had cost them too many lives. Now that Chaska was within reach of the chiefdom, if he survived his wounds, he didn't want anything to do with having the responsibility of being chief. He would also risk having the power go to his head. A man just never knew how he would be affected until he was put in that position.

# WREAK THE WRATH

LEVI JOHNSON WAS UTTERLY AWARE THAT HE WAS responsible for part of the problem with the Sioux. He was the one who spooked and ran off their horses, even though they had come there to kill them all. It was a bold move, and he was sure it left many warriors embarrassed before their peers. He was also aware that was not what this was all about. If so, they would have waited longer.

Beaver believed the Sioux chief had gotten the idea in his head of dominating over the land they lived on—land Sioux Chief Black Cloud had never even seen. It was for his ego and to leave a legacy—something of paramount importance to the leaders of most tribes. Many men who wielded such power thought they were God's gift to earth. Most, but not all.

This was the same, no matter what race they were. Greed for power was one of humankind's downfalls. With the White man, it was first greed for money; the greed for power came when they had more money than needed. It was similar in the world of a Native American

Indian chief. First, they fought for their tribe and honor. Then, once they were chiefs and they were showered with praise and gifts, it went to their heads, and they began to think they were someone they weren't. Delusions of grandeur infected their souls.

When the mountain men heard the alarm bell ring, they all grabbed their guns and rushed out the doors. It was instantly apparent why somebody rang the alarm bell. Flames lashed out the window of the stables.

When Rusty Steel stormed out the door, he yelled, "Dag-nabit, I knew that Ely Grimms was up to somethin'. They've done set the barn on fire, and I bet they stole the horses too." He didn't notice the silhouettes in the shadows at the side of the cabin.

"Check the horses!" Levi yelled as everybody moved at once.

"Start getting buckets to put the fire out," Dennis shouted. "We can take water from the water barrels beside the cabin."

Forrester looked up at the barrels he had set up for their shower. Both were large and full of water. They filled them and let them sit in the sun to warm up before a wash. In the winter, they would make do with a quick wash of their faces and hands. Bill ran for the shed where they had the water pipes and grabbed a handful with fitters.

He ran a pipe from the shower water to beside the stables in three minutes. This allowed them a constant flow of water, filling buckets as fast as they could empty them. Luckily, they caught the flames early, and there wasn't much straw in the stable. They put out the rest of the cinders with the last drops of water in the shower barrels.

"Come on, Forrester," Levi yelled, trying to keep up with Rusty as he recklessly raced down the narrow trail.

The mountain men were furious and wanted blood. They imagined things would be missing from the cabin, along with the missing horses and mules. Johnson hoped the hunters hadn't found their gold coins from the Rendezvous.

Suddenly, Rusty skidded to a stop and stooped to check the dead body beside the trail. "He's done killed his brother," he whispered unbelievingly.

"Maybe Leroy didn't die all on his own either," Angus said. "I know Green Leaf was mighty suspicious; he went just like that after seven days. Especially right after that fool was in there alone with 'im."

"We best be more careful now, boys," Dennis said as he sniffed the air. The acrid smell of blood filled his senses. "We've got more men dead ahead."

All eight men followed their barrels down the trail and into the dark. On foot, they didn't make a sound, and as they knew this trail like the back of their hand, they shot down it like bullets. They stopped to smell and listen every five minutes, then roared down the trail again.

"Lord, have mercy," Dennis said when they encountered the dead Sioux. Arrows protruded from everything.

"What are Sioux Indians doin' back over here again?" Angus asked.

"This looks like Hachta's doing," Rusty said. He pulled an arrow out of the ground and said, "That be a Crow arrow. I reckon they bushwhacked 'em. The Sioux and the buffalo hunter got caught in an ambush."

"I believe they were after us again," Forrester said.

"It's logical in a military sense. We never expected them to attack again so quickly. That was clever. They were probably going to storm us just before dawn like they planned to do last time. What must have happened is the Crow discovered the Sioux while they were busy with something else."

"Over here's the something else," Rusty said. "Ely Grimms is shot full of arrows. One, two, three, four, five, six in all. He looks like a pincushion. I figure we're being watched right now."

"I don't smell nothin'," Levi said.

"Me neither," Dennis added.

"I don't see nothin' either, but I know Hachta is out there trying to decide what to do with us. You out there, Brother Hachta?" Rusty shouted. "Come on; I know you're there."

Soft sounds of horses' hooves were heard in the dark. Ten Crow warriors rode toward the White men. Their faces were painted, making them appear even more fierce. They stared with hostile eyes, their mouths no more than gashes.

"I knew it had to be you," Rusty said. "It's about time you ran those Sioux off your land."

"It's not my land, Rusty Steel," Hachta said. "It is not your land either. We only take care of it for the next people to come after us. That is why it is so important to cherish it and give it tender, loving care. I killed the White buffalo hunter. Are you angry?"

"Me, angry?" Rusty replied. "Heck, no! Not for killin' this sorry excuse for a human being. As a matter of fact, I thank ya kindly. He just stole our horses and mules. You ain't seen 'em wanderin' about, have ya?" Rusty smiled knowingly.

Hachta looked at Rusty for a long time without saying a word. It was like he was trying to decide what to do. Finally, he looked down at his hands as he leaned on his saddle horn and then looked up and into Rusty's eyes.

"Yes, we have your horses and mules," Hachta said. "A bunch of beaver pelts too. You have treated us well in the past and lived with my cousins. We won't take your horses. We will take the White man's body with us, though. My chief will want to see his body after I take his scalp."

"Wear it well, Weasel," Rusty said right before the Indians vanished as quickly and as silently as they came.

"Whew, I don't wanna do that again," Forrester said. He was sweating bullets.

"I thought they seemed like mighty nice folks once you get past the war paint." Levi laughed. He was turning into a young Rusty Steel. It was happening right before Forrester's eyes, and Johnson apparently didn't even realize it.

"Let's get them animals back," Levi said.

"I need a drink." Rusty grinned. "Maybe even two."

# A Look at Book Three:
## Wolves Gold: A Western Double

**Gold stirs the hearts of men—but in the Rockies, it can also wake the wolves.**

**Wolves Gold**

Levi Johnson and former army Captain Will Forrester know how to survive the unforgiving winter wilderness. But when rumors of a hidden gold strike light up the settlements, the mountains grow crowded with greenhorns chasing riches—and drawing predators, both two-legged and four.

With winter coming fast, Levi and Will stumble on a dangerous mix: strangers tracking treasure, a pack of starving wolves on the move, and the first sparks of a powder keg ready to blow. Some say fortune favors the bold—but in these parts, it's the prepared who live to see spring.

**Outlaws**

The miners are gone, but trouble never stays buried for long. Two deserters from the army flee into the Rockies, dragging their pursuers right into Crow territory. Working as bounty hunters, Captain Holmes and Marshal Wilson chase justice through rugged terrain—only to blunder into a camp of sixty warriors.

Now, the fate of all involved lies in the hands of the tribe's elders. Loyalties are tested, truths are put on trial, and the fragile peace between mountain men and

*AVAILABLE JULY 2025*

# ABOUT THE AUTHOR

Ash Lingam was born and raised in Southern Ohio, not far from the mighty Ohio River. He had somewhat of an isolated upbringing on a family farm with his sisters. His best friends were his horse, Sugar, and his grandfather.

Born in 1886, the family patriarch grew crops, raised cattle, and doted on the young boy. At his grandfather's side, Ash learned about livestock and firearms at an early age. His grandad carried an old Colt with him at all times. It helped spawn a young boy's dreams of yesteryear.

Ash was only eight years old when his grandad taught him how to trap muskrats to prevent them from draining the farm's ponds. He gave him a double-barreled shotgun at twelve and taught him how to hunt to put food on the table.

It wasn't long before Ash was breaking horses. His spirited Tennessee Walker never allowed any other rider on her back. Together, they searched through the plowed fields in the spring, looking for Miami Indian arrowheads to add to his grandfather's ample collection.

Ash's family was among the early settlers in pre-

Revolutionary America. He has traced his lineage back to around 1746 when his ancestors immigrated from Europe to the aspiring American Colonies.

A retired marketing executive, Ash devotes his spare time to training police dogs and writing novels. He has found his niche in the Western, historical fiction, and adventure genres. With his vast vault of experience, he never runs out of sources for new stories. He has lived in eleven different countries and worked in a total of forty-six to date, Ash has written approximately 130 novels, short stories, and poems. More than one hundred of his eclectic titles help the American frontier come alive for his readers.

https://www.ashlingam.com/
Join the Lawless Waters Western Readers & Writers
Facebook Group